The Gre...
and the King of
Shadows

The Green Lady and the King of Shadows

A Glastonbury Legend

Moyra Caldecott

Gothic Image Publications
Glastonbury, Somerset
1989

The Green Lady and the King of Shadows
A Glastonbury Legend

Copyright © by Moyra Caldecott, 1989

First published in this version by
Gothic Image Publications
7 High Street
Glastonbury
Somerset BA6 9DP

Printed and bound in Great Britain by
The Guernsey Press Co. Ltd., Guernsey, Channel Islands.

British Library Cataloguing in Publication Data

Caldecott, Moyra, *1927*–
    The green lady and the king of shadows.
    I. Title
    823′.914 [F]

ISBN 0–906362–11–3

For Mary
With my love and gratitude

Other books by Moyra Caldecott

Novels in print:
GUARDIANS OF THE TALL STONES (a trilogy set in Bronze Age Britain)
Arrow 1986
THE SILVER VORTEX (sequel to GUARDIANS OF THE TALL STONES)
Arrow 1987
THE TOWER AND THE EMERALD (a trilogy set in Dark Ages Britain)
Arrow 1985
ETHELDREDA (set in 7th Century England)
Arkana 1987
CHILD OF THE DARK STAR (set on another planet where the astrologers
have made a rigid caste system)
Bran's Head Books 1984

Novels out of print:
THE LILY AND THE BULL (set in ancient Minoan Crete)
THE SON OF THE SUN (set in ancient Egypt, Akhenaten)

Non-fiction in print:
WOMEN IN CELTIC MYTH (retelling of legends plus an analysis of esoteric
meanings)
Arrow 1988
Three short books retelling Celtic legends published by Bran's Head:
THE TWINS OF THE TYLWYTH TEG 1983
TALIESIN AND AVAGDDU 1983
BRAN, SON OF LLYR 1985

To be published:
THE AMUN TRILOGY: DAUGHTER OF AMUN (Hatshepsut, female king of
Egypt c. 1473–1458 BC) Arrow June 1989
THE SON OF THE SUN (Akhenaten c. 1353–1333 BC. Previous version
revised and extended) December 1989
DAUGHTER OF THE SUN (Tutankhamun and his wife c. 1333–1323 BC).
Arrow 1990
All obtainable from Gothic Image, Glastonbury.

CONTENTS

It did not seem strange to him that he, Lukas, existed on many levels of time and space simultaneously; that the mysteries of his past were even now present and working through him without his conscious knowledge. He realized that we do not cease to live in the Spirit Realms because we live on earth. We may forget and need reminding from time to time just how complex and magnificent being human is, but we never lose our true capacities no matter how far we drift away into carelessness and ignorance.

INTRODUCTION:

I BELIEVE THAT myths and legends, while appearing to be pure fabrication hallowed by constant repetition, actually have their roots in a deep and abiding truth that can only be expressed through symbol and allegory. As a substratum of the main truth which is universal, there often lies a stratum of a more local and literal truth, an ancient event or belief that sparks off a chain of linked stories about a particular place. Many legends suggest that Glastonbury Tor in the sixth century was the scene of a confrontation between the old religion and the new. In an imaginative fusion of several crucial legends from Glastonbury's past I hope to give some insight into the living truth that they, together, illuminate.

The setting – Glastonbury, Somerset – has been described by Anthony Roberts in his book 'GLASTONBURY: Ancient Avalon, New Jerusalem' as 'an enchanted area of land – that generates and guards a powerful magic . . . the symbol of a great and holy mystery'. Frances Howard-Gordon, after asking why so many myths and legends are associated with Glastonbury in her book 'GLASTONBURY: Maker of Myths', concludes: 'there is a certain quality about the place, in the weird and wonderful landscape, in the peculiar shade of light, in the air we breathe . . .'

It is not for nothing that Glastonbury has continued to be a place of pilgrimage for so many centuries – that generation after generation have sought the secret meaning of their lives there – that today a visit to it is a 'must' for anyone interested in the dawning of a New Age in this troubled and crippled world . . .

THE HERMIT STRAIGHTENED his back and looked up, the axe still in his hand. He had been chopping logs for some time and had begun to feel his age. He thought for a moment he saw a dark shadow move in the forest to the side of him and turned his head quickly. There was no movement now, but he could not shake off the impression that he was being watched – and not by an animal.

He put down the axe as quietly as he could and his hand went to his belt where a flask of water hung – holy water from the Sacred Well – a weapon more effective than any axe against the kind of enemy that threatened him.

It seemed that he stood a long time there – tense, ready.

There was no further movement.

The sun reached its zenith and a shaft of light suddenly blazed through the leaves of the forest canopy and almost blinded him. When it passed on the feeling of another's presence was gone too.

Collen relaxed and started to gather up the logs of wood in his arms.

LUKAS COULD HAVE sworn the earth had moved beneath his foot.

He stood still, staring in alarm at the apparently firm greensward of the apple orchard.

He had known this orchard for years, ever since he had come to the monastery. Why had it moved? How could it possibly have moved? The earth was immovable, unchangeable, the beautiful anchorage of his life. His father had died. His mother had died. Even the walls of the church were taken down and rebuilt from time to time. But the earth with its covering of deep green grass, rich in cowslip and daisy, was surely there for ever.

After staring at the ground for a few moments he convinced himself that he had imagined it. Above him in the branches of the trees the birds sang and fluttered. They were not alarmed. Nothing had changed for them.

He took another step.

The earth gave way and, with a shout of astonishment, he fell down a huge hole that had suddenly opened up beneath him.

'Mother of God!' he gasped, smarting and terrified, struggling with the loose earth full of wriggling worms and fibrous roots that had fallen with him. He fought hard to get a grip on the lip of the hole and haul himself out, but the more he tried, the more the lip gave way, and more earth and grass joined the mass already in the hole.

At last he paused for breath and, finding that in fact no one was attacking him and he was not in any great pain, he looked about him to try to decide what had happened. Apart from the mound of earth that had come in with him he saw large stones that appeared to have been roughly squared and fitted upon one another to make the floor, walls and ceiling of a tunnel. The smell that came from the darkness was so musty that Lukas could not but think that it was very old and had been closed for a long, long time.

The fear that had come with the shock of falling had passed, and he now felt only excitement. He had discovered something that no one else in the monastery knew about. At last he had something that was his own, that need not be shared. He had come to the monastery as an orphaned and homeless boy and had drifted into a novitiate as he grew up. Now as a young man he was approaching the taking of his first vows without any great conviction. He would be a monk out of gratitude for what the monks had done for him and because he scarcely knew another life. There were times when he experienced a deep and intense sense of mystic reality, but mostly his life was hard work and routine shared with a hundred or so other men who held everything in common and who implicitly obeyed the rule of the Abbot.

More and more recently Lukas had found the routine of the monastery irksome, particularly the lack of privacy.

He thought back upon the stories he had heard about the Tor, wondering if there had been anything about a tunnel, but he could remember nothing. There had been other tales, tales of demons sighted on the summit, tales of mysterious hounds heard howling in the air at night or in a storm, tales of boats seen approaching the island through the mists and yet never seen landing – all cited by the abbot as being proof that the ancient religion that used to be practised on the Tor was the work of the devil, and dismissed by Brother Peter of the kitchen as superstitious nonsense. But no one had ever said anything about a tunnel.

Lukas' days at the monastery were divided mostly between working in the kitchen under Brother Peter, peeling and chopping food, scouring iron pans, stoking fires; working in the scriptorium copying texts; singing in the choir. There was a rota system for the choir so that there was not a moment of the day or night when the chant of praise to the Lord was broken or interrupted. The perpetual choir had been the idea of a previous abbot and had been intended as a flow of beautiful and harmonious sound that would lift the hearts of the imperfect, earth-bound creatures to unite with the perfect choirs of heaven. The present abbot had kept up the practice not for any such noble motive, but because he loved custom, regularity and routine. In spite of that, the deep, rich sounds of the chant of praise never failed to thrill Lukas and some of his happiest moments were, paradoxically, those when he was least alone, his 'little' self totally transcended in union with the angels as he sang in the choir, or when he was most alone, working in the vegetable garden or the orchard, his thoughts his own.

Now, crouching in the tunnel, he wondered how to keep his discovery secret. He stacked the squared stones that had fallen from the ceiling carefully and, climbing on these precarious steps, stretched and struggled until at last he scrambled back into the fresh air and the familiar green orchard. He checked the position of the sun and knew that it would not be long before he would be expected for his duties in the kitchen.

He looked at the hole. Although it had seemed huge to him as he fell, it was not really so large and, luckily, it was well to the side of the main orchard in a place so overgrown with brambles and weeds that not many people came that way. It was for this very reason he had chosen to be there, often yearning for privacy in the relentlessly communal life of the monastery.

He dragged fallen branches from the wood that bordered the orchard, and tugged and pulled until he had a makeshift cover for the hole. He wanted to be sure he would have a chance to explore the tunnel before anyone else found it. He didn't know what he expected of it – but whatever it revealed or wherever it led he wanted to experience it alone, in his own way.

THE FOLLOWING DAY a fowling expedition took Lukas away from the monastery and the orchard.

They set off in three shallow punts just after the earliest dawn prayers. The coming of light brought sound and movement to the water lands and there was the rustle of small rodents from the bank, the splash of fish leaping and falling back into the meres, the call of bird to bird on the wing, and occasionally the honking of a wild goose.

The party was in the charge of Brother Andrew who knew that he had a great many mouths to feed at the monastery and must return with a good supply of fresh meat for the cook. He intended that they should penetrate deep into the marshes before they started hunting. Lukas was in the third punt, moving quietly behind the others, enjoying the peace. Their pace was leisurely enough for him to enjoy the soft hush of the sedges as they stroked the sides of his boat, while the feathery flower heads of the reeds he touched shook above him, the pollen from them drifting like fine gold dust in the air. He saw pink orchids and purple gentian quietly pushing the grass stems aside on the little islands and wished that he had time to explore. He thought of living on an island by himself, providing his own food, dreaming his own dreams, poling his own punt when he felt like it. He forgot about the cold winter mists and the clammy ghosts of departed souls he might encounter, the wind and the icy rain flattening the reed heads, the snow flurries and the crackling ice. Summer always seemed as though it would last forever when it was there, and as though it would never come back when it was winter.

'What were you doing yesterday?' his companion, Matthew, suddenly asked. Lukas was startled out of his reverie. He remembered the tunnel.

'Why?' he asked sharply.

'I was looking for you and I couldn't find you.'

'I was in the orchard.'

'I looked there, but I didn't see you.'

'Just because you don't see someone it doesn't mean that they're not there.'

Lukas could see that keeping his secret from Matthew might well be more difficult than he had thought. The boy was fourteen, but a very small and sickly lad. He had somehow made Lukas his hero since he had defended him on several occasions against bullying, and tended to follow him about like a dog its master.

The young man frowned as he lent out of the punt and pushed at the reed covered bank to extricate it from the mud. He had not been concentrating on the water as he should and had come in too close. The other boats were already out of sight. Should he tell Matthew about the tunnel? It might be easier in the long run than trying to keep it hidden. Of anyone he knew Matthew would be the only one with whom he would enjoy sharing a secret. But if Matthew were cornered he might tell the others. A secret in a community where they were all bunched together with very little privacy might serve to buy him importance, a temptation Matthew might not be able to resist.

'Take the pole,' he commanded. 'Push that log.'

Matthew eagerly took the pole and pushed. His arms were like sticks. He was proud to be asked to help, but no matter how hard he worked, the boat did not break clear.

'Come, give it to me,' said Lukas impatiently. The punt rocked dangerously as he moved beside Matthew and leaned out as far as he could, the pole gripped in both hands. Matthew watched as Lukas pushed. His hero was tall and strong. His admiration for him knew no bounds.

9

The punt was dislodged at last, but by this time the other boats were nowhere to be seen. The plan had been for the three to stay close together until Brother Andrew gave the signal, and then Lukas and Matthew were to create a disturbance so that the wild duck would rise from their hiding places in the reeds. Cerdic, a sullen, heavy-set youth, and Brother Andrew, would then shoot their arrows. The other boat would retrieve the kill. The monks never used more than three punts, for one direction must always be left open for the birds to escape if they could.

Once clear, Lukas poled hard, weaving in and out of the little islands, avoiding mud banks and rotting logs. The daylight was growing stronger every moment and he began to fear that they were lost. As he rounded each bend, each cluster of tall bullrushes, he was sure that he would see the others. But there was no sign of them. He decided to find an island and chose one that had a bit of height to it. He waded ashore while Matthew looked after the punt, and climbed through the tangled weeds to its summit. From there he had an extensive view over the vast expanse of flat marshland. To the east there were hills on the far horizon but in the immediate vicinity was nothing but flat marsh and the one sudden, extraordinary hill, the Tor, the abode of demons, rising from the forests clinging to its sides. As Lukas looked at it he was almost blinded by the blazing golden light of the sun rising behind it. He shut his eyes quickly, but even through the smarting and the watering, he could see an after-image of glory that made him gasp.

'Is anything wrong?' called Matthew as he saw Lukas stagger slightly and cover his eyes with the palms of his hands.

Lukas shook his head, but he felt very strange, as though he at that moment was someone else, seeing the Tor in a different way, influenced by different memories.

But as suddenly as the strange feeling had come, it went, and he turned his attention back to the low-lying marshlands and scanned for any signs of the other two boats. At first he saw nothing and then he noticed the reeds shaking to the south-west. Suddenly, as though a handful of seed had been scattered in the air, a flight of frightened ducks arose, heavily beating their wings and crying their long sad cries. The scene was distant but Lukas could make out the sudden break in the composite pattern of their flight. He saw the falling of limp bodies, and heard the calls of the hunters.

'We might as well go home,' Lukas said as he rejoined Matthew. 'The others seem to have managed without us.' He climbed into the boat and pushed off without another word, his face clouded. Matthew watched him anxiously, sensing that something had happened on the island, but did not know what.

Lukas was thinking about the Tor, the strange and magical Tor that both frightened and fascinated him. It rose, mysterious and compelling, to the east of the untidy cluster of wooden buildings which comprised the monastery. Its lower slopes were forested but its summit was strangely flat, bare and windswept. Many were the stories of hauntings he had heard about the Tor, and no one of the village dared visit it. There were legends that in the ancient days when his people were still pagan, the island on which Glastonbury monastery was built had been the gathering place of all the spirits of the dead and the Lord of the Underworld waited on the Tor to greet them.

Four times a year, at the turning points of the seasons, the monks wound through the forest, circling the base of the Tor, chanting prayers of exorcism but never, as far as he knew, climbing to the top. When Lukas was a boy he had decided that when he was a man he would march boldly right up to the top of it and see for himself if any of the tales were true. Now it seemed, if his tunnel led where he hoped it did, he might well learn its ancient secrets in a different way.

THREE DAYS PASSED before Lukas could go back to the tunnel, but when he did he was well prepared. He wore his sheepskin jerkin against the clammy cold and carried rushes dipped in tallow for light and a sharp kitchen knife against the dangers he might meet.

He spent some time reinforcing the lid of branches and twigs he had fashioned, so that it could be drawn aside easily from the inside of the tunnel as well as from the outside. He did not want company on his secret expedition.

The rush light made weird flickering shadows and for a moment he hesitated to take the first step into the unknown. If the roof had fallen once, might it not fall again? What creatures lurked in the depths of the earth? He shuddered, remembering dark stories he had heard of monsters in underground caverns and tunnels. But in the stories they usually guarded treasure. What treasure might he not find in this dark place? This island had been inhabited since very ancient days. Old bones had been found, flint arrow heads, small carved stone heads from pagan times – even golden bracelets and necklaces. The chalice they used for the Eucharist each morning was made of gold melted down from ancient artefacts found in the earth not far away.

Lukas found that he was sweating, though even in his jerkin he was very cold.

'Fool! Idiot!' he muttered to himself. 'Those are just old stories!' But he went slowly forward, holding the flame of his torch well above his head, feeling with his left hand the knife at his belt and the sheaf of spare rushes strapped by a thong of hide to his back.

The light flickered wildly on the damp and crumbling walls as his hand shook.

'Stupid!' he said aloud, and then looked sharply over his shoulder as his voice came back to him as a hollow whisper.

He had the impression that he was in the presence of a very powerful force – whether for good or evil he could not tell. It was as though he could feel the tremendous energy of the earth, coiled, waiting to spring; the energy that pushed huge oak trees out of tiny seeds, that raised mountains out of plains. And it seemed to him that the energy was conscious – was conscious of *him* – was in fact watching him in some way . . .

It was as dark behind him now as it was ahead. He moved quickly, determined to find out where the tunnel led and to return to the comforting sunlight as soon as possible. But as the icy moments went by and there was nothing but the rough stone and the clammy darkness, his heart grew heavier and heavier and he began to have second thoughts.

'I'll come another day,' he told himself.

He turned, his shoulder brushing the wall and displacing the dust of centuries. The flame of his rush was burning low but its light momentarily caught a marking on one of the stones, the first mark of any kind that he had noticed on the walls. He lit another rush from the dying one and with the brighter light examined the marking. It seemed very old, blackened by the same time that had darkened and mouldered the blocks of rock out of which the tunnel was built.

He rubbed the grimy surface with his sleeve, trying to see more clearly what the mark was, but as he put pressure on the block of stone it moved. Alarmed, he jumped back and turned to run, but his curiosity was now stronger than his fear and he paused. He held the light close to the wall again and pushed the marked stone, poised ready to retreat if necessary. But this time, although again it moved slightly under his hand, it did not give so easily.

He tapped the wall and found that it gave back a hollow sound. He knew that he could not leave until he had found out what was beyond it. He put his rushlight on the ground, propping it up against the bundle he had been carrying, so that its light was aimed directly at the wall. He slid his knife blade into the fine cracks around the marked block and began to scratch and dig.

Gradually the rock loosened. He pushed and pulled and scraped until his knife was blunt and his fingers were bleeding, but at last it had sufficiently swivelled on its base for him to get a proper grip on it. He tugged at the stone and suddenly the huge block came loose and began to fall. He tried to hold it but he was not strong enough and leapt back only just in time as it hit the stone floor, the sound it made reverberating like thunder down the black and dismal tunnel.

Was it he who screamed with fear or something else in the shadowy darkness behind the stone? He would have run then if he could have but fear seemed to have turned his legs to dust and he could not move. The jolt of the fall had knocked the rushlight over and its flame now set the whole bundle alight. Suddenly flames flared upwards and illuminated the tunnel like daylight.

Lukas stared with horror as the shadow of a giant towered over him. Shuddering, he turned to run and then realized that it was his own shadow, magnified by the leaping flames, the same flames which now brought light to the dim cavity behind the stone that had fallen. He gripped the grimy sides of the hole and peered fearfully in. Briefly and brilliantly what was beyond was illumined.

13

He stared into a dark cavern, its walls dripping with slime. In a far corner a ghastly grey figure lay, chained by a metal that gleamed like gold, to the black wall. A figure that lifted its skeletal head to look at him as he stood framed in the hole he had made.

He ran, stumbling and cursing with terror and pain as he knocked himself against the walls, back the way he had come, each step taking him further and further from the flaring light of the bundle of rushes, and the dreadful thing that lay in the dark hole beyond the marked stone.

'What's the matter with you?' Brother Peter asked, startled as Lukas almost fell through the great door of the kitchen, his eyes staring and his face and clothes smudged and dirty.

Lukas looked Brother Peter blankly, for the moment not knowing what to answer, only half realizing where he was.

'I . . . I fell,' he stammered out at last.

Brother Peter looked at him long and hard. Had he been brawling again? Only last week in defence of the young boy Matthew, Lukas had been involved in a fight that could have turned really dangerous if the Brothers had not stopped it in time. Would he ever be controlled and disciplined enough to please the Abbot and be finally accepted into the Order? Sternly he pointed to the ash bucket and the pile of greasy pans to be scoured and then left the room. Normally this was one of the most unpopular tasks in the kitchen but today Lukas set to it with a good will, relieved to have some ordinary, practical thing to do to make him forget the extraordinary experience he had just been through. Never would he go down that tunnel again; never lift that lid of branches. The only thing he would do was return to the hole the next day when the sun was full and bright and pull great boulders over the entrance to block it up so that no one would ever find it again, and no one or no 'thing' could ever climb out of it.

He thought about Brother Peter. He was a gentle man. He kept his helpers busy and allowed no slackness, but he did not shout and punish as some of the other monks did. Everyone obeyed him out of respect, not out of fear. Should he confide in Brother Peter? Perhaps that 'thing' needed exorcism. But when Brother Peter returned to the kitchen he was in a hurry and told Lukas to be off.

Walking away slowly the troubled young man remembered the

words that had been read aloud in the chapel that morning.

Out of my distress I called upon the Lord;
the Lord answered me and set me free.

He whispered them over and over to himself, wishing he had the
certainty of faith Brother Peter seemed to have, wanting to believe the
monks' teaching, but not finding that the way the Abbot taught it rang
true to his own experience.

That night Lukas lay a long time before he could sleep, although his
body was more weary than it had ever been before.

The dormitory in which he slept was a long low room, the roughly
trimmed tree trunks which held up the beams of the thatched roof
covered with clothes at night hanging from inumerable pegs driven
into the wood. The beds were rough trestles and very hard, the
blankets hand-woven in the monastery from wool spun from their own
sheep. In winter they had sheepskin rugs they had cleaned and cured
themselves – all except the abbot who had a bear-skin brought with
him from the mountains of Wales.

Although in the east and the north of the country enemies had
overrun their land and every day the danger of an invasion by the
Saxons grew greater and greater, the monks kept their community in
the old Celtic way as it had been for centuries. They prided themselves
that there had been a monastery at Glastonbury before the Romans
came to Britain, and it was still there long after they had left. They
believed the same would happen should the Saxons come. They would
absorb the invader, tame him, and watch him go. Had not God himself
led Joseph of Arimathea to this very place after Our Lord's death and
given His promise that their tiny island would be an inspiration to the
world for millennia to come? The original wattle huts which Joseph
and his twelve companions had built had long since rotted, as a man's
body must rot with the passing of time, but the spirit of the work they
had done still lived. In the Scriptorium, by the light of smoky mutton-
fat candles when the sun was gone, the monks copied the gospels on
vellum and sent them by river and sea, over mountain and plain, to far
away places where others could read them. In the little chapel, half
built of stone, half of wood, by night and day, a perpetual choir sang

15

the praises of Our Lord and asked, as He had said we must ask, for help and guidance and protection.

The four seasons turned and turned again like a great wheel; battles were fought in distant places; kings rose and fell; but the work of the monastery went on at the centre as though it were a still point in Time.

Lukas lay on his hard bed and listened to the steady rhythmic breathing of those around him. The monks worked hard and were grateful for sleep when it came. Usually it was only Matthew who had restless nights. Lukas could hear him now, wheezing in his sleep. As though he could feel Lukas' attention on him, the lad turned over in bed and started to cough. Lukas lay in the dark and listened to him. When would that cough end? Matthew had been brought to them the autumn before so ill with fever that no one had thought that he would live. But he had recovered with the monk's care, prayers and herb lore, to take his place among them. But sometimes his small frame seemed to be about to burst with the violence of his coughing. Lukas shut his eyes and whispered a prayer for Matthew as he had many, many times before.

Gradually weariness got the better of Lukas and he drifted off to sleep.

In his dream he fell again the long fall to the darkness beneath the earth, and walked unwillingly the passage he had walked before. No matter how hard he tried, he could not turn back.

As he approached the hole in the wall where the marked stone had been he noticed that light glowed from within the cavern and in spite of his fears he found himself peering through the hole. He could see the grey figure more clearly now and found to his surprise that it was not such a fearsome sight as he had at first thought. It was nothing but the frail form of an old, old woman chained to the wall, and as he stared at her she stirred.

He looked at her steadily, strangely no more afraid, and met her eyes. She seemed alive, but tired and sad beyond belief. She spoke no words to him, but her eyes asked for help with such a burden of pain in them he would have tried to help her had it meant facing the hounds of hell.

'I will help you!' he cried, pulling at the rocks around the one already dislodged, trying to make the hole large enough for him to climb through into the cavern. The relief in her eyes was so beautiful that for a moment he was convinced that he saw not an old woman upon the floor, but a young woman of great beauty and delicacy, with gold hair falling almost to her feet . . . a woman he seemed to know.

He stopped what he was doing in amazement, but even as he did so the vision faded, and he awoke with a start in the long dormitory, Matthew and the others still sleeping on either side of him.

He stared around him, puzzled. The dream had been so strong and vivid he could not believe that it was only a dream. Unlike other dreams, the memories of which slithered away as soon as wakefulness came, this one was so vivid he remembered every detail of it, as though it were something that had really happened to him.

He realized that he was no longer afraid of the cavern and what it held. The girl reminded him of moonlight, fine and silver, shining on water on a summer's night.

He lay for a long time thinking about her, feeling a kind of ache, a stirring, a restlessness – a longing to touch her – to know her as woman – to experience what it would be like . . .

He tossed and turned trying to get away from the seductive images that came to mind . . . trying to find some explanation for her presence in that place.

He must go back and set her free.

And he must go back alone.

IT WAS NOT until the late afternoon of the following day that Lukas found the opportunity to escape to the orchard. He had managed to arrange it so that everyone who would have expected him to be in one place now expected him to be in another, and so no one knew precisely where he was at any given moment. He had a sudden qualm that if anything horrible happened to him in the tunnel no one would know where he was and he would probably be buried alive, lying there, undiscovered for centuries. He shuddered. Was this what had happened to the woman he had seen? He thought of Mathew. He could swear him to secrecy, but then if he were just a few moments late for Vespers Matthew would panic and tell everyone. No, it was better that he told no one. On the other hand . . . Lukas wasted precious moments wavering. In the end he decided on a compromise.

In the Scriptorium there were various pieces of smooth slate stone the abbot had brought from Wales. On them those who had been chosen to be scribes practised their letters before being allowed to work directly on the vellum. Lukas had several small broken pieces in his possession. He slipped to the place behind the kitchen where he had hidden them and scratched a message for Matthew on one of them. 'Look for me where you could not find me. But this time under the earth.' He thought that that was sufficiently enigmatic to hide his whereabouts from the others and yet clear enough for Matthew to find him if necessary. He returned to the dormitory and slipped the piece of slate into Matthew's bed. Hopefully he would be safely back to remove it before it was found.

Finally Lukas turned his attention to the orchard and his secret tunnel.

He had, as he had planned, bread and water with him, but a suitable cloak had been too difficult to find. The loosely woven blanket from his bed was folded and fastened over his shoulder, the hammer and chisel from the workshop, with his stock of rush lights and his knife, were in his belt.

It was good how confident he felt as he walked the way he had walked so warily before. The dream was still with him and he felt no fear. He even whistled softly to himself as he moved deeper under the hill.

A great deal of time seemed to pass and he could not help thinking that it was taking longer than before to reach the place where he had seen the woman chained; but he had noticed before how one's impressions of time altered with mood and circumstance. Perhaps he was imagining it. He paid even closer attention to the wall at his side. Eventually he retraced some of his steps, afraid that he might have missed the hole he sought. But there was no sign of any break in the hard wall and he continued forward again. Surely he should have stumbled over the great stone on the passage floor even if he had missed the hole itself? His light slithered over the rough stones ahead of him, revealing nothing.

He began to feel more and more uneasy. He *must* have passed the place! He stopped short. Was he mad that he had believed so absolutely in a dream? What had made him do it? Never before had he trusted those fragments of insubstantial mist that clung about him as he slept. Never again would he. And then he started as he heard a faint sound ahead of him. He strained his ears to catch it, but the darkness pressed silently upon him again and he could hear nothing.

He turned on his heel, thinking to return the way he had come. It was as thought he could feel a cold breath on the back of his neck.

He heard the faint sound again and he paused trying to decide where it was coming from and of what it reminded him. It was a kind of faint rumble, becoming stronger and then fading at regular intervals. He held the rushlight high with sweating hands, peering into the darkness almost as though he expected to see the noise itself rather than what was causing it. This time he thought that there was something familiar about it. He strained a few paces nearer, listening.

'Sweet Jesus!' he suddenly gasped. He did recognize it! It was the distant muffled sound of a man chanting one of the monastery prayers. Relief flooded his heart. The tunnel must have come full circle and he was back at the monastery! He thanked God that he did not have to retrace his steps through that fearful gloomy tunnel and hurried forward, rejoicing as the sound of the prayer grew louder. He did not know the voice, but that did not worry him for it would be distorted by the hollow tunnel. He even smiled to himself at the shock he would give the Brother as he suddenly emerged. He no longer cared if the tunnel was a secret or not. He never wanted to come down there again.

Without his being aware of it the ground must have been rising all the time, for now it seemed he was at wall level, and not below the floor as he would have expected. Where the sound of the man's voice was loudest he noticed a small fissure of light. It did not take him long to find loose rocks to push and pull beside it. He noticed that the voice ceased when he started to scrabble at the rock and he knew that the man must be shocked and frightened by the sound of someone trying to break through the walls.

'I hope he doesn't attack me, before he sees who I am,' Lukas thought, and gave one last push.

For one second the small, bearded, ginger-haired man standing in front of him stared, and then before Lukas could properly recover his balance from his precipitate appearance, he lifted a pewter bottle that stood on a low table and flung the icy contents full in his face, shouting something in Latin angrily at the same time.

Lukas staggered back, gasping and spluttering, trying to wipe the water out of his eyes. The hermit stared at him for a moment, his eyebrows like untidy straw above his startled eyes, and then he seized a bowl from the same table and flung the contents of that as well. This time it was warm gruel.

'What in God's name do you think you are doing?' cried Lukas.

The man paused with a book in his hand, presumably intending it to follow the water and the gruel.

'What do you think *you're* doing?' he demanded.

'I found a tunnel. I thought I was back in the monastery.' Lukas gazed around him, puzzled. The room he was in did not look like a room at all. It looked like a hut of wattle boughs built against the side of the hill, the one wall half bedrock and half built of blocks of stone very similar to those in the tunnel. It was in fact an entrance to the tunnel which had been long since walled over, the hut built against it centuries later, and inhabited by a hermit.

'Nothing is as it seems,' the man said gruffly. 'You ought to be more careful.'

Having recovered from the shock of Lukas' arrival the stranger's eyes now went to the hole in the wall and he uttered a very irreverent exclamation of anger.

His presence took some explaining and Lukas did his best to make amends for the fright he had given him by telling him some, but not all, of his experiences. The man listened intently, grunted and then demanded that he leave forthwith and never enter the tunnel or his hut again.

Lukas was not sorry to go.

The forest was close about the hut. Behind it the slope of the Tor rose steeply. A tingle of excitement ran down his spine. That he should be so close to the mysterious mound!

The path the hermit indicated he should take almost instantly disappeared beneath an arch of green foliage and he was once again walking in a tunnel, but this time it was a green and living one. Trees

20

joined branches above his head, while their trunks wove together with bushes and flowers to make an almost solid wall on either side. The sun was low and the light fairly dim on the path, but when he emerged at last on Chalice Hill he saw the sprawling buildings of the monastery not far beneath him brilliantly lit by that strange bright, dying light of evening, the huge old oaks that stood like sentinels around it casting long, long shadows. 'Different light makes all things different,' Lukas thought. 'I am seeing something new though I have seen it a hundred times before.' The sound of the Vesper chant rose to meet him, and he began to hurry, suddenly realizing that he had been away a long time, much longer than he had intended. He wondered how many people had missed him; how many people he would have to explain his absence to. He dropped his blanket and his tools in an out-of-the-way shed to be collected later, and slipped into the chapel hoping to take his place at the back without being noticed. But the door creaked and there could not have been a person in the chapel who did not swing round and see him creeping in, shame-faced and dishevelled.

At the end he was called by the Abbot and went before him in some trepidation. The Abbot was an intolerant man, known to have had wrong-doers beaten for less an offence than Lukas had committed. He caught Brother Peter's eyes as the other monks filed past him and he knew that, though Brother Peter was curious as to where he had been, he would have been happy to accept any reasonable excuse he was prepared to offer.

But the Abbot trusted no one. He enjoyed imposing discipline. He had never approved of the custom begun by the previous Abbot of taking in orphaned children or those born out of wedlock and abandoned. Girls were always sent into the care of a sister monastery near Wells, but boys were brought to Glastonbury. In return for their keep and education a prince would have been proud to have, they helped the monks with the chores that the running of such a large community inevitably necessitated. Many, like Lukas, who had been taken in some years previously as a boy, stayed on intending to become monks themselves. These the present Abbot particularly distrusted.

He glared at Lukas and Lukas shifted uneasily from one foot to the other. What excuse should he make? This man was very different from the peppery but kindly hermit or the gentle Brother Peter. It had always seemed to him that the Abbot nursed a grievous and festering bitterness, as though his religion had spoiled his life instead of making it richer and more fruitful.

'The Lord does not like being kept waiting,' the Abbot said coldly.

'I am sorry Father, forgive me.'

'Forgiveness is for the Lord,' the Abbot said, 'after true repentance. You will stay on your knees outside the door of the chapel without moving, without food or drink, asking forgiveness, asking to be allowed back into the chapel. When the Lord decides that you have truly understood the privilege of attending His worship in His House He will admit you.'

Lukas caught his breath. When the Abbot said 'the Lord' he meant, of course, himself. Lukas had known him to keep a monk three full days and nights outside the chapel in this way. When they had finally been sent to release him from his penance he was unconscious.

Lukas cleared his throat. 'I . . . I was on the Lord's business, Father,' he said hurriedly in a low, hoarse voice.

The Abbot eyed him malevolently.

'And what business was that?'

'I . . . I met a holy hermit living on the side of the Tor . . .'

He was quite startled by the Abbot's reaction to his words.

'A hermit on the Tor?' he snapped – whether in anger or surprise it was difficult to tell.

'Yes, Father.'

'His name?'

Lukas shook his head. 'I don't know, Father,' he muttered.

'What did he look like?' barked the Abbot.

'He was short and stout, with red hair and a red beard.'

Lukas could see that he need say nor more: it was clear that the Abbot knew very well whom he was describing. His expression was agitated – but with a jerk of his hand he dismissed Lukas from the room.

'You can be sure the Lord had no hand in that meeting,' he said. 'Your penance begins now.'

'Father . . .'

'Now!'

The Abbot's rigid finger directed him to the door, and Lukas, with a bitter heart, went out. He was already weary and the ground outside the chapel door was hard.

'What does he know of the Lord?' he muttered to himself. 'If the Lord walked through the door this very moment he would not recognize him!' He wondered at the man's agitation and the dark and brooding shadow that he saw on his face as he left.

In the early hours of the morning when every bone in his body was aching and even his thoughts had ceased to go round and round in circles of resentment, Lukas drifted into what started as a reverie but later took on such a potent visionary aspect he could not be sure it was not more real than reality itself.

It seemed to him he was once again in a barque gliding through the marsh mists. This time he was seated and someone else was doing the poling. He could see the dim outline of a figure standing in the prow, guiding the barque forward. He thought at first it was Matthew, but the figure was too large. He leant forward, trying to see who it was, but the mist swirled between them and he could distinguish no features. He thought of climbing forward to take a closer look, but was too !ethargic. He relaxed, leaning back on comfortable cushions stuffed with aromatic herbs – wondering only idly why he felt no damp or cold, nor heard the splash of water as the punt pole worked the muddy depths.

After a while the barque came to ground and the ferryman half turned to beckon him. Even now he could not see the man's face, but he obeyed without question. He noticed that the barque did not rock as he rose to his feet and walked its length, and when he reached the prow the mysterious ferryman had disappeared. He seemed to be alone as he stepped ashore.

He stood for a moment on the fine white pebbled beach, peering through the mists, wondering where he was . . .

He thought he caught a sound at last and strained to hear it more clearly. As he did so he began to recognize that it was singing – faint and far-away but meltingly, hauntingly beautiful. For a moment he thought it might be the perpetual choir at the monastery, but the voices were high and delicate, and he knew that there were not enough young boys in the monastery choir to produce such a rich and soaring sound. The melody was different from any he had ever heard, lighter and merrier . . .

The mist seemed to be lifting and he was beginning to be able to distinguish faint smudges which reminded him of trees. He left the barque and walked forward in the direction of the singing – feeling remarkably light-hearted and unafraid.

The obscuring mist had all but disappeared as he reached the limit of the white beach. He could now see two trees before him quite clearly, their branches intertwined to form an arch through which he felt compelled to go. Beneath them a stream of clear water flowed and he had to step on mossy stones to traverse it.

As his shoulder brushed against a low-hanging branch, a tinkling sound made him look up. He was surprised to see that the leaves were crystals, each catching the light which now blazed down from a cloudless sky. The iridescent colour-play almost dazzled him, the whole a shimmering, sparkling cloud of light.

He hardly knew whether to look down at his feet to ensure that he did not miss his footing on the stepping stones, or to gaze upwards at the magnificent kaleidoscope of ever-changing leaf-patterns. He was in one of those states, so difficult to describe to others, where he felt he was somehow more than himself. He was expanded. He was loosened like a boat that had lost its mooring rope and was drifting free of his own bodily shell. Words . . . The memory of words he had once heard drifted past him like flotsam . . .

'. . . *the pure river of water of life, clear as crystal, proceeding out of the throne of God . . . and on either side of it the tree of life . . . the leaves of it for the healing of the nations . . .*'

Was this from the Book of Revelations, the magnificent vision of the New Jerusalem the angel gave to Saint John on Patmos that he had copied out so patiently so many times in the Scriptorium? Or was it from a tale he had heard long ago before he had come to the monastery, from a travelling Irish story-teller, about how a man had entered one of the mysterious mounds left by the ancient pagans that lay here and there upon the land, and to do so he had to pass between two trees of crystal and drink from a sacred stream . . .?

He stooped down and scooped up some of the water in his hand and drank it.

On the other side of the great arch of leaves he seemed to be in the fairest land he had ever seen. Never had he witnessed so many flowers blooming at once, so many fruit trees bending with the weight of their crop. The light was unusual – as gentle as moonlight and yet with the power of sunlight. It seemed to emanate from the ground and from everything around.

He could still hear the singing but it was a great distance away. More immediately he was aware of the notes of a flute weaving a thread of silver sound and enchantment around him. He looked for the source and saw a young woman clad in green seated under a hazel tree. A woman, so beautiful that, as he approached her, he was unable to take his eyes off her. Surely he had seen her before? Surely she was known to him? But he could recall no woman as exquisite as she in the humdrum life he had lived. She was like a princess in an ancient tale . . .

As he drew nearer she put down her flute and rose to her feet, smiling, as though she knew very well who he was.

It seemed to him that as he stood before her, looking into her eyes, he was falling back into a familiar role. Everything about her pleased him – the tilt of her chin, the delicate line of her nose, her long and silky hair, her softly rounded body. Her answering gaze was deep and warmly intimate. He had the feeling that he was a bird returning safely to its nest after battling through a storm.

He reached out his arms to her, overwhelmed with desire.

For a moment she looked as though she would come to him but something made her hesitate, he sensed a shadow cross her face.

She drew back and turned away and it as as though the very light in the land had dimmed. Was that a cool breeze that had arisen or was the chill he felt one of foreboding?

She was walking away across the meadow.

He followed her, hurrying, trying to catch up with her. Though it seemed she walked quite slowly, he found himself no nearer her.

He began to run, his longing for her now almost stronger than he could bear. He wanted to call out, but he couldn't remember her name. He couldn't remember his own.

They entered a wood and the trees crowded in around them. There were times when he couldn't see her, and he was almost in despair. Then he caught a glimpse of her and stumbled on in pursuit.

She appeared now to be carrying something on her hip. She was moving differently, her step no longer so springy.

For a moment she paused and allowed him to see her more clearly.

She turned towards him and for the first time since she had retreated from him he looked into her eyes. She was different, older. She was carrying a young child on her hip and at her waist hung a heavy ring of keys. Her face and figure were fuller, more mature. It seemed to him he had come home after a long journey and she was waiting for him beside the hearth. But even as he reached out for her once more she turned and moved away, disappearing through the trees.

Again he followed. Again he couldn't reach her.

He could think of nothing else but that he must be with her. He could not – would not – go back without her.

Go back? Where to? He had forgotten who he was and how he came to be where he was.

And then he glimpsed her clearly once more for a moment – she was now an old woman, bent almost double. And then, suddenly, there was no trace of her. He searched frantically. It seemed to him the meaning of all things would become clear if only he could speak with her. He had desired her body when she was young, her comfort when she was middle aged, and now he desired her wisdom.

And then he remembered the woman chained in the cavern beneath the Tor. He remembered the monastery – the apple orchard and the tunnel . . . He remembered his name.

'That is where I'll find her,' he thought triumphantly, 'back in my own time, my own place. That is where she is.'

He turned to retrace his steps and found that the forest had vanished – the beautiful land had gone. He was lying on his face on the ground at the door of the chapel and Brother Peter was shaking him by the shoulders.

'Quick!' he was saying. 'The Father will release you now, but he must not see that you have been sleeping!'

Lukas had never heard the chapel bells so loud and discordant.

Sleeping?

6

THE NEXT DAY Matthew was taken ill after a particularly vicious piece of bullying by Cerdic. Lukas stayed close and busied himself with his duties. Gradually the vividness of the experience he had had began to fade, and he started to believe more and more that he had been dreaming.

But on the third day, restless again, his thoughts turned back to the mysteries of the tunnel, the woman chained there, and the young woman he had followed in that magical land. Illusion or not, the experience had been disturbing.

The Tor itself rising clear and bare above the forest began to pull him like a lodestone. He could not help thinking that the secret of the woman buried in the tunnel beneath the Tor, the woman he increasingly longed to see again, must be connected in some way with the stories of the hauntings that surrounded that peculiar hill. He found himself going more and more to the place in the monastery grounds where he could see it. And the more he stared at it, the more the stirring in his heart responded to it. On the fourth day he could bear it no longer. He determined to climb the Tor and face whatever lay in wait for him there.

He managed to persuade the duty master to assign him to garden duties and as soon as he could, he slipped away. He had kept his oatbread from breakfast and slipped it into a small pouch at his belt. He did not make for the tunnel entrance in the orchard. This time he set off confidently in search of the path that would lead him to the hermit. But it was not as easy to find as he had hoped. After several false starts he eventually found what he thought was the right track through the forest. Sometimes it was easy to follow, at others it disappeared altogether and he had to search his memory very closely for images of leaf and branch, of flower cluster and unusual rock to guide him in those places where the path petered out. He was overjoyed when he found himself at last in the green tunnel and knew that he was almost within hailing distance of the hermit. He wondered if he should speak with him, or hurry on? But the decision was made for him. When he reached the hut it was empty.

He continued past the place and upwards towards the Tor. All seemed ordinary enough, but as he climbed further up the slope he began to feel a little strange. He found he was not climbing directly up the hill as he would have expected, but was winding round and round it, occasionally finding himself apparently doubling back, yet on a higher level than he had been before, following almost imperceptible ridges in the earth. While he was doing this he felt no weariness at all, but as soon as he decided to break away from the ridges and cut directly up the slope to save time, he felt his legs were made of lead. Something seemed to be dragging him down.

'Nonsense,' he told himself firmly. 'The direct way must be quicker. I'll keep to that.'

But it was not quicker because each step had become such an effort. It was as though he were pushing against something in the earth.

A picture came into his mind as clear as though it hung before him in the air. He saw the image of a spiral maze burning like molten gold, turning through mist.

He stopped short. Something stirred at the side of his eyes. He swung his head round quickly to see who or what it was. There was nothing there but the trees and the rocks, though he could have sworn he felt a presence.

He shut his eyes and shook his head, trying to dislodge the disturbing image. When he opened them again he continued his progress directly up the Tor, but his heart was now as heavy as his legs. This was not the way. He knew it. Something was telling him to return to the place where he had left the ridges and follow them again.

'No,' he said aloud. But his unease grew, and his sense of potential defeat waxed so strong, he turned at last and retraced his steps to where he had left the faintly marked ridge path.

From then on the way was easy. He walked lightly and confidently forward, led up and up the hill, turning with the curve of the earth, following its natural rhythm to the top.

Suddenly the trees that had kept his vision close about him gave way to open space, and he paused with astonishment to see the landscape laid out before him in such splendour . . . his own forested island giving way to water and quiet reed beds . . . beyond these, long reaches of flowering marsh with occasional islands as richly forested as his own . . . and in the far west the silver gleam of the sea.

His heart lifted with joy. Surely this high hill was the centre of the world, the place from which all else flowed?

'You have not reached the top,' a voice that was not his own seemed to speak within his head.

Two more turns of the strange labyrinthine path and he would be at the very top.

How many times had he circled the hill? He had lost count.

His flesh began to tingle with a faint premonition. He looked uneasily around him.

The sun was high and by now his presence at the monastery would have been missed. He should return, but he found that he could not. The compulsion to go on having come so far was too strong. This was no ordinary hill and he must know its secret.

He looked up to the summit, knowing that if he walked through the tall wind-blown grass he could be there within a few moments. But he chose to keep to the path that had held him this far, and spiralled the hill twice more before he stood at last upon the highest point.

He had the feeling that this place was at once familiar to him, yet alien too. The monastery seemed very far away, the rules that governed its days and nights and that he had believed were so inevitable and inexorable, now appeared arbitrary and mutable – the petty and rigid repetition of its rituals out of step with the complex and subtle harmony of the universe.

Filled with an overwhelming feeling of triumph and excitement he flung himself down upon his back. Above him the immense dome of blue seemed to move, to wheel. Blood beat in his temples. Beneath his body the great earth turned. He could feel it, the earth turning, the sky turning, one within the other. Visible and invisible the realms of Being turned upon each other with a deep harmonious rhythm, more complex and more beautiful than anything man had ever dreamed of in his tiny cage of bone.

Transfixed with the power and beauty of it Lukas wished that he

29

would never have to move, never have to go down to the valley again, to the mindless violence of people like Cerdic and the cold authority of the Abbot.

He shut his eyes. The boundaries of things, the separation of one thing from another, ceased to exist. It seemed to him that he could feel what it was to *be* earth and sky, fire and ocean. He seemed to be 'inside' the Abbot's head, 'inside' Cerdic's, 'inside' the head of the reed-cutter he could see far in the distance wading up to his thighs in water. He felt the frustration of the first two as they battered themselves against the constricting walls of their own small egos, unable to break free into the wider realms of their true being. He felt the peace in the heart of the reed-cutter who knew nothing of the world beyond his village and this marshland, yet inhabited a greater world than either Cerdic or the Abbot. He felt the pain of warriors in battle, the sorrow of a mother holding a dead child in her arms. He shivered with excitement and awe, understanding in that brief moment, that we are not just what we seem but carry in ourselves the life of the whole universe, secret and revealed, natural and supernatural. Whatever happens in the universe, happens to us!

And then he felt he could bear the intensity of such a vision no longer and he leapt to his feet, looking around himself, hoping to see everything returned to what he had come to believe was 'reality'.

'I am Lukas!' he shouted, thumping his fist on his chest. 'And,' stamping his foot, 'this is the earth!'

Something moved to the left and he spun round to find, to his embarrassment, that he was not alone. Behind him on the Tor stood a stranger, a tall man, taller than any he had ever seen before. Around him a black cloak floated like a mist. His gaze was penetrating and sardonic. His stance majestic.

'So you are Lukas?' he said with perceptible amusement. 'And this,' he said pointing downwards, 'is the earth?'

Lukas reddened.

The man threw back his head and laughed. There was no mirth in the sound and Lukas felt no answering levity rising in himself. He shifted from foot to foot, wondering if he dare leave.

Was that thunder he heard in the distance?

He looked round to try to gauge how quickly he could get to the shelter of the trees and be out of sight, if the man decided to follow him.

He took a step back and the man, still looking into his eyes, took a step forward.

Lukas, remembering what he had been told about demons on the Tor, turned and fled, falling and sliding and slithering down the long slope to the forest. He forgot the spiral path, and broke his way through its ancient patterning, straight and sore to the base of the mount, and to the hermit's hut.

The red-bearded man was a stranger too, and yet Lukas felt him to be a friend. To his relief the small, stocky figure was working on his woodpile, swinging the axe as though he were a warrior in battle. He looked up at once when he heard Lukas' call and stared at him in some surprise, slowly straightening his back.

Breathlessly Lukas told him he had been to the top of the Tor. It seemed he need say no more. The hermit fetched a low stool from inside the hut and indicated that Lukas should sit. He then brought a pitcher of water, which to Lukas' relief, he did not throw at him, but held carefully for him so that he could drink.

Lukas was flushed and sweating, his legs and arms badly scratched from the forest thorns and twigs. He drank gratefully and when he had done the man brought a cloth and dipped it in the water so that he could wipe the blood and dirt from his cuts and scratches.

'You saw something on the Tor?' the man asked with more than ordinary interest, watching him carefully.

'I saw someone,' Lukas replied.

'Who?'

Lukas shook his head.

'What was he like?'

'Tall and dark and thin. He . . .' Lukas paused. How little his description fitted the man!

'He . . . what?'

'He did nothing. But I felt afraid of him. I ran away. It seems foolish now.'

'No, it was not foolish,' the hermit said grimly. 'You did the best thing. You were not ready for the encounter.'

'Who was he?' Lukas, now no longer afraid, was very curious.

The hermit did not reply, but seemed to be deep in thought. Lukas waited for what seemed a long time and then could keep silent no longer.

'What is his name?' he demanded.

The hermit looked at him, annoyed. 'His name is of no importance,' he said sharply. 'You don't ask me *my* name, and yet you ask me his?'

'What *is* your name?' Lukas said hastily. The man pursed his lips as though in two minds whether to reply or not.

'My enemies call me "old firebrand",' he said at last. Lukas laughed outright, the name was so appropriate. And then he straightened his face.

'Why do they call you that?'

'Because I can't abide fools,' the hermit snapped, 'and my fists have spoken for me on occasions when I ought to have used words.'

Lukas could believe it.

'What then do your friends call you?'

'Collen,' replied the hermit.

'May I call you Collen?'

'Brother Collen.'

'Brother Collen,' Lukas said politely. 'Will you tell me the name of the man on the Tor?'

'No,' replied Collen.

Lukas looked at the short, elderly man with the untidy red hair and the shaggy eyebrows which seemed to point in different directions. His eyes were small as hazel nuts and as bright as polished bronze. He could not help but like the man. He trusted him. If he would not tell him the name of the stranger on the Tor he must have good reason. He wondered if he should mention the woman in the tunnel, but he still could not bring himself to do so.

'If I know the Brothers, they will be looking for you by now, and mighty annoyed not to find you. You must go,' Collen said firmly.

'May I come back?' Lukas asked.

'Would it stop you if I said "no"?'

Lukas laughed. 'No,' he said.

'Well, then,' said Collen, 'be off with you!'

Lukas hurried off, but when he reached the turn of the path and he knew that he would not see the hut again that day, he swung round to wave. Brother Collen had the three legged stool in his hand and waved it at him.

Lukas smiled. He had a warm feeling in his heart where before there had been a cold and frightened one. Collen was of the world to which he was accustomed.

The Brothers were looking for him but not with the anger he expected. As soon as he appeared in the kitchen Brother Peter took him by the arm and led him out again, his face more troubled than angry. Lukas' mind raced to think of an excuse for his long absence and had decided to tell him about his visit to the hermit, though not about his climbing the Tor, when he realized that Brother Peter was not accusing him of anything and not asking for an excuse.

'What is it?' Lukas asked, suddenly alarmed. They were moving towards the infirmary and Brother Peter's face was anxious and sorrowful. 'Matthew!' thought Lukas. He was ashamed that he had been so obsessed with climbing the Tor that he had completely forgotten how ill Matthew was. It is true the monks had said that he could not have visitors, but Lukas knew they would have made an exception for him if he had insisted. Sin of omission! he told himself. So that is what that means! Now, it might be too late.

'Matthew is very ill,' Brother Peter was saying. 'We think . . . we do not think that he will live much longer.'

'But he is still alive?'

'He has been asking for you continually. We couldn't find you.' Brother Peter for the first time shot Lukas a sharp look. Lukas could not have felt more guilty had he been before the Abbot on a charge of mortal sin.

He put his head down and hurried forward. What could he say? That he was sorry? How inadequate that word seemed.

The beds in the infirmary were larger than the bunks in the dormitory and Matthew looked very frail, a small hump in the middle of a sea of blankets, his eyes seemingly the biggest things about him. Lukas stood looking down at him and felt a lump come to his throat as he listened to the boy struggling for each rasping breath. But when Matthew opened his eyes it was as though the sight of Lukas transformed him. His whole face lit up.

'What's this?' Lukas said gruffly. 'I hear you have been pestering the brothers for me.'

Matthew tried to say something, but was too weak. He appeared to

33

be trying to get his hand out from under the bed-clothes. When he finally managed it Lukas could see that he was clutching the little piece of slate that Lukas had forgotten to retrieve since he had first put it under Matthew's pillow.

'I don't know what it is,' Brother Andrew who had been in the room when they arrived, said. 'He has had it in his hand ever since he came here and he won't let anyone take it from him, nor anyone see it.'

Lukas put out his hand and Matthew with relief let the little piece of slate go. Lukas looked up at Brother Andrew. Brother Peter was hovering at the door.

'Could we have some time to ourselves?' he asked. The two monks instantly withdrew.

'They . . . they've been saying all sorts of prayers about death,' Matthew whispered.

'Well, you can't die yet,' said Lukas firmly. 'I need you.'

'Need me?' sighed Matthew and smiled such a beautiful proud smile that Lukas cursed himself for all the time he had wasted in not taking the boy into his confidence.

'Yes,' he said. 'All sorts of strange things have been happening to me . . .'

'I thought so,' breathed Matthew. He looked at the piece of slate now in Lukas' hand. 'What does it mean?'

'It means I have found a tunnel that goes right under the Tor. I didn't want anyone else to know about it, but when I was going to explore it I thought I'd better leave a message where I'd be – in case – in case I didn't return.'

Matthew was listening eagerly. He was already beginning to look better. 'I thought it was the orchard!'

'The tunnel comes out in the forest almost on the side of the Tor through a hermit's hut.'

Matthew was hanging on his every word. Lukas sat on the edge of his bed and began to pour out everything that had happened – even his strange dreams. The sick boy took on new life as he listened. When Brother Andrew looked in a while later he was astonished to see how much better Matthew looked. He came in and stood beside Lukas.

'We must not tire him . . .'

'O, I'm not tired!' cried Matthew, but the effort of saying that started him coughing again.

Lukas stood up. 'I'll be back,' he said. 'You have to rest and get better.'

'You'll . . . cough . . . come back . . . cough . . . and tell . . .'

'Yes, I'll come back . . . and when you're better I'll take you to see Brother Collen.'

Brother Andrew looked at him quickly at that, but said nothing. Later Lukas was called before the three Brothers, Peter, Owen and Andrew, and questioned about Brother Collen. Lukas told as much as he had told the Abbot. The three monks looked at each other.

'It is indeed providential that you should have met him Lukas. He is known to have performed several healing miracles for our Lord.'

Lukas was astonished. Brother Collen did not look like a saint, and as far as Lukas knew, only saints performed miracles. But if there was any chance of making Matthew better they must certainly take it. Brother Peter asked him if he would fetch the hermit in the morning.

'Of course, but . . .' Lukas paused. He was puzzled as to why they had not called on Brother Collen themselves for Matthew, and indeed why he had never heard any of them ever mention him before.

'It is a long story Lukas,' said Brother Peter reading his expression. 'And it is not altogether a happy one. One day we will explain, but for the moment it would be better if you were the one who asked him to come to Matthew. But go now. Eat your supper. Pray for young Matthew. Sleep.'

Lukas left, ate his supper, prayed for young Matthew and prepared himself for sleep.

The dream he had that night had the same potent visionary quality that the others had had, but this time he was not in the tunnel, nor the cavern where the woman lay, nor the mysterious land beyond the crystal trees.

He walked again the long and winding path that spiralled round the Tor. But this time the ridges seemed more definite, built up like walls of earth. They were not very high, but high enough to prevent his crossing over from one path to the other as easily as he had done the previous day.

It did not seem strange to him that he now knew that the spiral had seven turns. In fact every moment things were becoming more and more familiar to him as though he had been to this place under these conditions often before.

He was part of a procession climbing the Tor along the special path. In his hand he held a bare branch. The forest trees around him were equally un-leafed.

As the head of the procession turned to disappear behind the hill he saw that the young woman of his vision was leading it. Behind her flowed a cloak of shimmering green. Upon her head was a ring of silver. In her hand she also carried a branch.

He wanted to hurry, to catch up with her, and to speak with her, but he could not. He was held back by a sense of awe, by a sense of what was fitting and what was not.

He looked round for Brother Collen and the nameless man he had seen upon the Tor, wondering if they would be somewhere in the procession. But there was no sign of them. All were strangers and yet . . . and yet . . . he felt he knew them all.

As he came to the last turn of the path before the summit he looked up and could see that the head of the column had already reached it. He could not see the young woman, as the people were forming a circle around the edges of the flat top of the Tor. He could just make out her bough held high as though she were standing in the centre of the circle.

A heron winged slowly over him, a messenger from other worlds.

Suddenly he seemed to remember, to know something about himself that made him gasp. He was not only Lukas who lived in the monastery, scrubbed pots and sang in the choir, he was someone else, someone with a strange name, Gwythyr, son of Greidyawl, and he had lived long, long ago, and in that other life he had been chosen to represent the Sun in ritual marriage with the Earth.

All around him now the people were drawing aside and urging him to move forward. All eyes were upon him, all hands guiding him to the centre of the circle where the girl stood, the girl whose name was Creiddylad, the young and beautiful daughter of Lludd, chosen to represent the Earth.

Above the Tor the sky arched immensely vast and blue. No cloud darkened the amazing clarity. And in that blue, directly above them, the white disc of the full moon stood like a bride. The bridegroom, the burning Sun, stood beside her.

Gwythyr seemed to burn with the Sun's light as he moved forward to

36

stand before Creiddylad.

Everything fell silent.

Was it possible no birds sang? No one breathed?

How – or why – Life came to be was an ancient mystery, but the people he found he was part of in those ancient times knew that it could not happen without the male and the female, the sun and the moon, the spirit and the flesh. But male sky god or female earth goddess were not enough. It was in their union that Life received its impetus.

The girl began to turn, pivotting slowly on her bare heels, drawing him with her. Those around them began to do the same until, circle within circle, all were turning.

It was then he felt her touch and a running line of fire seemed to spiral from it, burning the husks and stubble of his old self to clear the field for the new planting. With their limbs entwined they lay upon the earth and it was the pulse of the earth they matched with the rhythm of their love-making. No nectar could have been sweeter to a humming bird than that which flowed between them. A hundred, thousand people could have been crowding round them but they saw nothing, felt nothing, but the enclosing warmth of each other and the thrill that ran through every part of them.

The landscape was changing. All the scattered sheets of water were transformed into shimmering whirlpools of light, the marsh lands and reed beds, the dark trees of the forests – all seemed to have become spirals of energy. The slopes of the Tor were covered with white flowers like a bridal veil. Buds were visibly unfolding, branches pushing out new leaves. The young woman's bough had become white with blossom, emitting a dazzling light that shot out across the country bringing rich abundance to everything it touched. His own bare branch was covered with fresh green leaves.

He shivered with the beauty of it all and the sadness that he must at last withdraw from her. With a sigh he shut his eyes to rest them from the intensity of the light.

When he opened them again, he opened them in the dormitory, and only the shadow of his shining experience was left, the memory of his ancient name already fading.

For the rest of the night Lukas tossed and turned, and could not sleep. Red-eyed at dawn he decided that when he went to Brother Collen he would tell him everything about the woman in the tunnel and about his visions. There *must* be an explanation. These were no ordinary dreams.

IT WAS A bright day of sunshine and blue sky when Lukas set off to fetch Brother Collen, and he was feeling confident and happy. He believed Brother Collen would be able to help Matthew and it was a relief to have made the decision to share the burden of his secret. He had not been walking for long however when he knew that he had taken a wrong turning: the blackened trunk of a tree that had been struck by lightning and was lying across the rough track had not been there before. He looked at the weathered upended roots and knew that they had been exposed to the air for a long, long time.

He felt suddenly cold, and when he looked up he found the sky was no longer blue. A chill breeze began to stir among the leaves.

Annoyed with himself for his carelessness, he turned and tried to retrace his steps. It was not as easy as he thought it would be and he cursed himself for spending the time composing speeches in hishead to make to Brother Collen when he should have been concentrating on finding his way. The track he was on twisted and turned torturously, branched frequently and gave him no clues as to which way to go.

Suddenly he glimpsed the Tor through a break in the almost continuous cover of branches and thought with relief that at last he would be able to tell in which direction he was walking. He was surprised how far away it appeared and decided to leave the treacherous path and cut directly across the forest towards it. In that way he hoped to strike the path that passed Brother Collen's cell and which led to the top of the Tor.

It was tiring work bending back brambles and bushes, wading through deep bracken, much of it still dry and prickly from the year before, and many times he had to retrace his steps to avoid an impenetrable mass of thorny branches.

The weather had turned cold and dark, and the forest was strangely silent. More than once he looked sharply over his shoulder as something seemed to move in the undergrowth behind him.

At last, when he was almost in despair of ever reaching the hermit's hut, he was startled to come upon a clearing, and in the clearing was an extraordinary building. Immensely tall tree trunks covered with carvings formed columns to hold the roof so high up it was almost out of sight. Images of twisting and interlacing animals and plants curled round each other on the wood, swallowing and regurgitating each other. Fishes with the heads of dragons, vines with tendrils of snakes, men so deformed that their legs were knotted behind their ears, women giving birth to monsters . . . Lukas stared at them all – appalled and fascinated by the sense of a rich and fecund power, a wild and dark imagination.

He rubbed his arms to try to keep warm, for the cold drizzle was beginning to soak through his clothes. How could this building have existed so close to the monastery and yet he had never heard it mentioned? And then he remembered that the hermit had not been mentioned either.

He stepped forward, full of curiosity, ignoring an inner warning voice.

With his hand almost on the door he heard a sound behind him and spun on his heel. He was looking into the piercing eyes of the man he had seen at the top of the Tor. The chill from the cold and misty air was nothing to the chill he now felt in his heart. He wanted to run, but stopped himself and tried to regain some of the sense of purpose and the confidence he had had in his dream.

'You were looking for me?' The dark eyes bored into his.

'I didn't know,' Lukas stammered, annoyed with himself for showing his nervousness. The eyes were watching him as he had seen the eyes of a cat watching a bird before it pounced. He had the impression that he was backing slowly, precariously along a log balanced over an abyss and at any moment he could fall off and be destroyed.

Suddenly the man smiled. 'You are welcome,' he said softly. 'It is a cold day. Why do you not join me at my fireside and share a meal with me?'

Lukas did not know what to do. There was no doubt that he was tired, and cold, and hungry. There was nothing he would like better than food and drink and somewhere to rest. But . . . there was that warning voice again deep in his heart. Brother Collen had refused to name this man. Why? He was desperate to know more about him. He had seemed so menacing on the Tor – but at this moment he did not seem so.

Lukas decided to accept, but asked his name.

'My name will mean nothing to you,' the man replied. 'It belongs to former times.' Lukas fancied he saw a shadow passing across the thin, gaunt face. 'Come, my food is nourishing, my fire warm,' he added. And he led him through the door.

Lukas noticed that a great many of the carvings on either side of him as he passed through were of heads with two faces, each facing a different way, each carrying a different expression. Seeing this, he hesitated once more. Why would the man not give his name?

'Lukas!' The stranger spoke sharply, and indicated that he should precede him into the chamber. Lukas obeyed. What he saw took his breath away. The place was huge and richly furnished. Upon a long low table a feast of many delicacies was laid as though an honoured guest was expected.

'Sit,' his host said pleasantly, and waved his hand towards a stool covered for comfort with thick and glossy furs.

Lukas stared at the hand that pointed. It had been bare when he had beckoned him to the house, but was now covered with jewels. The man himself seemed much younger, almost handsome in a hawk-like way. A cloak of darkness flowed around him.

'Who *are* you?' Lukas whispered hoarsely, now deadly afraid.

'I might well ask you the same question,' the man replied, looking closely at him from under lowering brows.

'You know my name.'

'That name is a broach you wear upon your outer garments. You can pin it on or take it off as you wish. It does not belong to your spirit.'

Lukas frowned, trying to recapture an image, or the shadow of an image, that, for a brief moment, he half thought he saw. But it was gone.

40

'Tell me who you are?' The man was gazing deep into Lukas's eyes as though he wanted to read what lay hidden in his mind.

'My father was a farmer named Joel, but he is dead. My mother . . .'

'You are wasting my time. These answers mean nothing. Tell me who you *really* are!'

Then it seemed to Lukas that he was beginning to wonder himself who he 'really' was. If he was no more than whom he had always assumed himself to be, how did he know the things he knew that no one had ever told him? He began to concentrate, remembering the experience he had had upon the Tor – the knowledge that had come to him so vividly of infinite motion, infinite stillness – of pattern and splendour beyond anything he had ever seen or heard tell of . . . He thought about the dreams he had been having – the name he had had in the dream – the name which he no longer could recall.

'I . . . don't know,' he said at last, hesitantly; and that was the truth.

The tall man rose and paced impatiently about the room. Lukas watched him as he put his jewelled hand to his mouth and bit the knuckles irritably.

'You must be someone I have known,' he muttered, pacing back and forth, back and forth. 'Otherwise why do you pursue me so?'

Lukas said nothing though he was surprised. If anything, he would have thought it was he who was being pursued!

'You are meddling with the tunnel. Why?'

'I stumbled upon it by accident.'

'Nothing happens by accident,' was the snarling reply. His eyes were sparking with dangerous fire and his mouth was twisted with rage. 'You moved the marking stone,' he continued. 'You saw the woman.'

'What woman?' Lukas was determined to deny everything, at least until he understood it better.

The man resumed his pacing. He seemed pre-occupied now with his own thoughts and Lukas took advantage of this to move towards the door. Several times he paused, afraid the man would notice and stop him, but it was as though he had been forgotten.

As he left Lukas could not resist taking a piece of fat and juicy meat from the table.

As soon as he was clear of the great house he looked back to see if he was being followed. He gasped. The magnificent structure he had seen

41

and indeed, had been inside, was no longer there. In its place was an ordinary hut, not much larger than Brother Collen's. The meat in his hand was a charred and evil looking claw.

In Brother Collen's shelter he was given food and drink while he sat upon a plain wooden stool without any covering of shining furs. The hermit watched him with affectionate amusement as he greedily ate the bread and berries, the hot soup and milk that he provided, and did not attempt to talk until he saw the colour back in his cheeks. And then he asked where Lukas had been and what he had seen to make him look so distraught.

Lukas told him he had seen the man that had frightened him on the Tor.

'Did you speak with him?' Collen asked gravely.

'Yes. He asked me who I was. He knew my name yet he kept asking me who I *really* was.'

'I have asked that question myself,' the hermit said in a voice so low it was almost inaudible.

'O no! Not you too!' Lukas cried.

Collen pulled himself together. 'Tell me what happened,' he said aloud.

Lukas shrugged his shoulders. What had happened? And where should he begin.

'Start with the day you came bursting through my wall.'

And so it came out at last, piece by piece, much of it muddled and confused, but at least it was the whole story as far as Lukas knew it. Collen listened to it intently and made no comment. At the end, he still sat silently, deep in thought.

'What do you think? Is there a prisoner in the cavern?' Lukas asked. 'I had thought it was my imagination until he mentioned her himself.'

'Did you tell him the story you have just told me?'

'No.'

'Anything of the tunnel, or of the Green Lady on the Tor?'

'I did not tell him, but he seemed to know I had been in the tunnel.'

'You did not tell him of your dreams?'

'No.'

They both sat silently for some time. It was Lukas who spoke first. 'What does it mean?' he asked.

Collen frowned, his eyebrows coming together like a single piece of ragged fox fur.

'There is much to unravel here Lukas, and I do not think we have all the threads of it yet.'

'But tell me something to help me understand,' Lukas pleaded.

Brother Collen shook his head thoughtfully.

'If I say what I think now it may all be false. Something is unfolding for you and it will take its own way, its own time. If I interfere now it may not run its full and natural course and we will be left worse off than we are now.'

It was frustrating, but Lukas could dimly see that what the man said made a kind of sense.

'Have you ever been in the tunnel yourself?' he asked.

'Once. But I did not see the marked stone or the cavern. To me it was nothing but a dark passage, well left alone.'

'Why did you build your hut against it?'

Brother Collen shrugged. 'Who knows? Perhaps I thought it might be useful to have a secret way of escape one day.'

'Escape from what?'

'One never knows,' he said enigmatically, and left it at that.

'Perhaps that is why I didn't want to tell anyone about it,' Lukas thought. 'Perhaps I too thought of it as a way of escape.'

And then he remembered Matthew.

Ashamed that he had delayed so long he told Brother Collen how the monks had reacted to his name and how they had asked for him to come to the monastery to help Matthew. The hermit pursed his lips at this and looked thoughtful. Lukas wondered if there was some kind of bad feeling between the monks and Collen, that something had happened in the past to drive them apart, and it would take an effort on both their sides to bring them together now. He hoped that they would do it for Matthew's sake.

He began to tell Collen about Matthew and how he was the only one in the world he had told his secret to before he had told Brother Collen himself. The hermit shook his head violently and for a moment Lukas feared that he was going to refuse, but then it seemed that the hermit was shaking his head as though to clear it of something. He stood up and stretched as though he were breaking his attention off from one matter, before he concentrated it on another. Lukas watched him with relief, knowing now that Brother Collen would not let him down.

Suddenly he began to feel very, very weary.

Collen saw it and smiled. 'Stay here,' he said quietly. 'Sleep awhile. I'll help your friend if I can.'

Lukas found his eyes already closing and he slid forward and rested his head on his arms on the table. Was this enchantment too as the strange house had been, or was it just the natural weariness of someone pulled from every side by potent and inexplicable forces?

He was not sure whether he was awake or not when he thought he heard Brother Collen say: 'Whoever you may be, sleep well.'

WHEN LUKAS AWOKE to find himself in Collen's hut he was at first surprised. Then he remembered. He looked around for the hermit, but there was no sign of him. How much time had passed he could not tell but there could be no doubt it was long past the time he should have been back at the monastery.

Greatly refreshed after his sleep he started back along the path, only to hesitate before he had gone more than a few steps to change his mind. He decided to return to the monastery along the tunnel. It was shorter and quicker and he would be able to have one more look for the marked stone and the mystery of the chained woman. He felt less frightened of doing this now that Brother Collen shared his knowledge.

The stones in the hermit's wall had not been disturbed since the day he had made his sudden appearance. He pulled them out carefully, struggling with the weight, wishing that Brother Collen was there to help him. He had understood from the hermit's words that it was somehow up to him, Lukas, to find out more about the mystery before any explanation would be attempted. Today he would try to do just that. He took Brother Collen's lamp, feeling sure that the hermit

44

would not object.

Once inside the dark, dank, confined space of the passage his resolution almost wavered, but he decided to go on. He moved slowly, swinging the lamp from side to side, determined not to miss the marking stone. Spider webs brushed against his face and made him start. A small creature scuttled away from his foot and he almost dropped the lamp.

It seemed the walls had no other carvings apart from the one he had seen. Would he ever find it? He stood still and thought about it. He tried to concentrate his mind, to send it like a beam of light into the dark to seek out the thing he wanted to find.

He began to feel strange, as though a power were growing inside him that he could not control. It was almost as though he could see in the dark and no longer had need of the lamp. He set it down and walked resolutely forward coming within a few moments to the mark he sought. He did not pause to wonder if the mysterious man who had fitted the stone back into the wall was near, but put his hand straight on it. This time, without pressure, it gave and swung open like a door. He entered the cavern and stared at the scene before him. The man he had first met upon the Tor was there, clad in his cloak of darkness and, facing him boldly, was a young woman in green.

Although she was still chained she was standing upright, fearlessly gazing into the man's eyes.

'You'll not win,' she was crying, her voice ringing clearly in the dark and hollow place. 'Death is your kingdom and only death you can reap. You have not won me by bringing me here.'

'Silence!' he roared, and his voice was fiercely angry.

He stretched out his arms for her, his shadow ahead of himself, touching the hem of her green gown. Shuddering, she crouched against the wall of rock, her face twisted away from him, golden rivulets of hair falling like a curtain between them.

Suddenly, Lukas knew who the man was.

'Gwynn, son of Nudd,' he shouted. 'You shall not have her!'

He found himself with a sword in his right hand and a hard leather shield grasped in his left.

The man turned and Lukas looked into the eyes of an ancient enemy. How many centuries had passed since the great god-king Arthur had doomed these two men to fight on the first day of Spring

45

each year, the girl Creiddylad torn between them until the Day of Judgement, life struggling with death, the fine and silver heir of Spirit challenging the dark Guardian of the Underworld?

Creiddylad, the woman whom they both loved too much, wrung her hands.

'Gwythyr,' she cried. 'You cannot win. Not here. Not in this Isle of Shades. Seek the sun . . . fight him in the sun . . .'

But Gwythyr, son of Greidyawl, had his sword at the throat of the man who had stolen his betrothed and cruelly slaughtered his kinsmen and friends.

'I lost to you once Betrayer of Trust! I will not lose to you again,' Gwythyr cried.

The King of Shadows raised his arms; darkness flowed from them and from the centre of the darkness Gwythyr saw his pointing finger and felt pain sharper than any sword pierce his heart.

He fell and as he fell, he saw Creiddylad reach for him – her eyes filled with love and pain and longing . . . but between the two of them there was a gulf of darkness widening every moment . . . and across this gulf there seemed to be no bridge.

'Lukas . . . Lukas! Where are you?' Brother Collen's voice broke through the strange buzzing in Lukas's head.

'Here,' his voice answered from what seemed a hundred leagues away. 'Here!' Here. But where was she . . . where was she . . . Creiddylad . . . the lady of light and life . . .?

'Why did you put down the lamp?' Brother Collen fussed. 'Why did you not wait for me?'

Lukas shook his head helplessly. Why? Why? Would there always be questions and never any answers?

He was in the tunnel, not the cavern. There was no sign of the marked stone or the entrance he had thought he had burst through. There was no sword at his feet. No feeling of power in his heart.

He sighed. 'I wish these things would stop happening to me,' he said. 'I wish I could be myself again.'

Brother Collen put his arm round his shoulder and gave him a comforting squeeze. 'Perhaps that is exactly what is happening,' he said.

'What?'

'You are learning to be yourself.'

'I mean myself – Lukas.'

Brother Collen looked thoughtful. 'What we are is more complex and more exciting than we think,' he said. 'He who grew up here on Glastonbury Island, who cleans the kitchen and waits at table, who studies Latin and sings in the choir, is only a small part of the Being who comes from God. We in our lives act out the Ancient Mysteries and no matter how small and insignificant we seem, in the secret inner levels of our Being, we are actors in the mightiest dramas of the Universe.'

Lukas looked bewildered.

'Never mind,' said Collen with a smile. 'This will become clear to you one day. Meanwhile, let's get you home to your friend Matthew.'

Lukas looked at him quickly, suddenly alert. Collen read the question in his eyes. He smiled. 'Your friend sleeps now. I think that you will find him much improved.'

Lukas could not find the words to say how grateful he was, but he did not need to. The hermit could see it in his face.

'What did you . . . I mean . . . how did you . . .?

'*I* did nothing . . . it was the grace of God.'

'But why . . . if it was God . . . why did he not get better with *our* prayers?'

Brother Collen shrugged his shoulders. 'He would have, if you had known how to pray. It is a matter of slipping out of yourself as you are in Time, into yourself as you are in Eternity.'

Lukas was silent, plodding beside the hermit as they made their way towards the orchard entrance of the tunnel. Should he ask the man to explain himself? He sighed. He thought perhaps he would leave it for another time when he was not so confused . . . besides . . . they had reached the pile of earth at the tunnel entrance and it was time to lift the lid of branches and climb out. Lukas was shocked to see that it was full dark already and the stars were shining through the apple trees. It had been a long and extraordinary day and he did not know what to make of it. One thing he was certain of – he was hungry and tired and longing to get back to accustomed things.

'Will you come back to the monastery with me?' Lukas asked Brother Collen. 'It is dark and probably dangerous to be walking about in the forests of the Tor.'

Collen laughed. 'Do not you worry about me. I'm as tough as an old root that can split a rock. No demons would dare pick a fight with me.'

Lukas believed he was right. Stocky and muscular and full of confidence in himself and his God, Brother Collen would be a match for the Devil himself.

'I'll say goodbye here then,' said Lukas. 'Will you . . . will I see you again tomorrow?'

'That's up to you.'

'I'll come over in the morning if I can. I . . . things happened in the tunnel that I must tell you about.'

Collen looked at him sharply, but any conversation they might have had was cut short by the bell for Compline, the monks' last prayer before retiring for the night.

BUT IN THE morning Lukas did not seek Brother Collen.

He lay most of the night puzzling over the strange things that were happening to him and trying deliberately to keep himself awake so that he would not have to live through one of those weird dreams again. He wondered if he were going mad and if Brother Collen had only been humouring him by listening so intently to his stories. He began to long for the simplicity of the life he had led before he had discovered the tunnel. Just before dawn he dropped off to sleep. He began again to feel as though he were drifting out from his body, leaving it lying on the bed while he, in some ghostly other guise, travelled through the night. He tried to wake himself up. He heard his own voice crying in his head and he strained every muscle to make his body sit up, shake itself awake. But not a limb, not a single finger, would respond to his commands. His body lay numb as though it were dead while the thinking part of him looked down upon it for a moment and then seemed to slide away into the dark.

48

He began to hear sounds. This time he was not in the tunnel, nor on the Tor, but riding on horseback through the night. He could feel the horse beneath him, powerfully galloping, feel the wind blowing in his face, feel something cold and hard at his side. He knew it was a sword. Behind him he could hear the thundering of hooves and turned his head to see the shadowy figures of his companions grimly riding behind him. One of them drew level with him. The night was full of stars and black shadows, the dark hills crowding in around them, echoing with hoof beats as they rode into a narrow valley.

'Gwythyr,' called the young man who was now riding at his side. 'It is better if we dismount and come upon them silently.'

'I'll sneak up on no one,' he replied proudly. 'The Lord Gwynn may come as a thief in the night – but I will fight a fair fight and win Creiddylad back the honourable way.'

'Gwythyr!' called the young man again, but Gwythyr impatiently drove his heels into his steed and drew ahead.

Ah! Kyledyr, son of Nwython, if only your friend and boon companion Gwythyr had listened to you that fearsome and bloody night!

Suddenly arrows were raining from the stars. Rocks were falling from the high-towered crags of the gorge through which they rode so carelessly. Gwythyr heard his friend's steed scream in agony and turned to help him, but in the dark milling whirlpool of horse flesh, cold iron and flailing arms he could not find him. Gwynn's men were leaping out at them from every shadow. His head was bursting with the shouting and the clanging of iron on iron.

'Gwynn ap Nudd!' he roared. 'Show yourself! Thief of women! Dishonoured among gods and men!'

But Gwynn ap Nudd did not show himself to Gwythyr son of Greidyawl that night, and wield his sword and turn his stallion as he would Gwythyr found himself at dawn alone in the gorge, half his men dead around him, the others taken prisoner by Gwynn.

Tears of rage burned in his eyes.

'Gwynn,' he screamed, beating his chest. 'Why not me! Why not me!'

But Gwynn had known that taking Gwythyr's companion as he had done would cause his enemy more pain than any wound, however deep. And Kyledyr, son of Nwython, Gwythyr's closest friend, the one he loved above all others, was Gwynn's greatest prize.

Suddenly Lukas jerked awake. Brother Peter was leaning over him, shaking him.

'Lukas, what is it? What is the matter?' the kindly monk called. 'Wake up! Wake up!'

Lukas began to shiver uncontrollably. He kept looking round expecting to see those awful corpses lying on the blood-soaked ground, but all he could see were rows of wooden bunks, pale light shining through the dormitory door and Brother Peter's anxious but friendly face above him.

'Kyledyr,' gasped Lukas.

'Who?' asked Brother Peter.

'Kyl. . .' but already the memory was fading, the name of his friend slipping from him. 'Matthew,' whispered Lukas. 'How is he?'

'Matthew is well enough,' the Brother said, smiling. 'We had not allowed him off his bed yet; but it will not be long.'

'May I see him?' Lukas found himself thinking about Matthew: but somewhere in the back of his mind a memory of another friend was tugging and teasing . . .

'Yes, of course you may see him. He has been asking for you.' Brother Peter was relieved that Lukas seemed now to be himself again. He had been called to the dormitory when the others had reported that Lukas was thrashing about in his bed, shouting and cursing in a voice very unlike his own, and could not be woken. The monk had said a prayer of exorcism and the young man had calmed down. When Peter was certain it was safe to do so, he had set about waking him. Now as he looked at Lukas's sweat-soaked hair and clothes he decided that he must have a quiet and uninterrupted talk with him at the earliest opportunity. Something was disturbing him. Something was very wrong.

When Lukas saw Matthew he asked him what he had thought of Brother Collen. The lad described how he had knelt down beside him and put his hands on his chest. 'It was very strange,' he said. 'I felt very peaceful and his hands became very hot and soothing. He just left them there for ages and I didn't cough at all. Just felt peaceful and hot and half asleep. I remember . . .' He paused.

'What do you remember? Tell me everything.'

'I remember thinking . . . about you . . . in the tunnel. I wasn't worried as badly as I had been, but I was a little frightened I suppose. I just sort of saw you in the tunnel with . . . with a lamp . . . searching. And when I thought this he . . . he said: "Don't think about Lukas in the tunnel child. I will see that he comes out safely. Think of the life you have been given . . . think what it means to have been given the gift of life." '

'You mean you only *thought* about me – and he knew what you were thinking?'

'Yes. He answered everything I thought as though I had said it aloud.'

'What else?'

'I was afraid suddenly . . . I had wanted to die because I felt so bad and because it seemed that I was nothing but a nuisance to everyone. Father Abbot said . . .'

'Forget what Father Abbot said!' interrupted Lukas fiercely.

'And then when Brother Collen told me to think about life I began to see all the things I wanted to do and I began to be terribly afraid that I would not live to do them. I remember thinking – I felt well now with his hands on me, but what if when he was gone that terrible pain and that cough came back . . . how could I bear it. "Don't be afraid," he said at once. "Never be afraid. Spirit is with you. Draw on its strength. Trust what it can do for you." '

'What Spirit? Did he give a name?'

'No. I remember thinking that myself . . . and he said at once: "If it will help you to give a name to that which is Nameless – do so – but never forget that what you have named is a Mystery powerful and potent beyond any words man can devise for it, and the name that you have named belongs to you and not to It." '

Lukas was listening, spell-bound.

'Are you sure you did not say these things aloud?' he asked.

'I am sure – because afterwards I asked Brother Owen and he said that I hadn't spoken at all the whole time.'

With the effort of talking so much now Matthew began to cough again: but Lukas noticed that it was by no means as severe and as prolonged as his coughing would have been the day before. He restrained himself from questioning Matthew further and sat quietly

51

beside the boy, busy with his own thoughts. It was Matthew who eventually broke the silence by turning the questioning round to what had been happening to Lukas. Slowly the strange events were described. When Lukas came to the dream of the galloping horses, the dark gorge and the sudden attack, Matthew began to shiver and look so frightened that Lukas broke off.

'What is the matter?'

Matthew shook his head and said that he didn't know; but it was clear that the story of the dream was finding an echo somewhere in his own far-memory.

'Go on. Go on!' he whispered eagerly. 'What happened then?'

'I remember being alone and the terrible feeling that it had been my own foolhardiness that had given my friend Kyledyr, son of Nwython, into the hands of . . .' The names came easily now. But before he could finish the sentence Matthew was sobbing and shaking.

'What is it? What is it Matt?'

'I don't know. I don't know,' sobbed Matthew. 'It is that name makes me feel terrible . . . O God, forgive me . . . I did not know . . . forgive . . . forgive . . .'

'Matthew! It was only a dream!' And in his anxiety to calm Matthew down he almost persuaded himself that it had been no more than a dream.

Brother Andrew came bustling into the room and found Lukas sitting on the edge of Matthew's bed, holding the young boy in his arms while he sobbed hysterically.

'What on earth . . .?' Brother Andrew rushed over to them and pushed Lukas aside. 'What have you been saying to him? I left him almost recovered and now look at him!' The sobbing had made Matthew cough uncontrollably again.

'I was telling him about my dream,' Lukas said.

'The dream that made *you* scream!' cried Brother Andrew angrily. 'Have you no sense?'

Lukas suddenly felt exhausted and utterly despairing. He was being moved by forces out of his control and something at the back of his mind stirred and tormented him . . . an old feeling of guilt . . . Kyledyr, son of Nwython . . . Why did these names ring in his head . . . ring in his head . . .

Andrew managed to calm Matthew down and gave him an infusion of nettle leaves to drink to soothe his cough, followed by camomile tea as a sedative.

'What he needs more than anything else now,' the hermit had said as he left, 'is sleep and rest. In a few days he will be walking about again. When he is a little stronger, I want to see him . . .'

It had been strange seeing Collen again, Brother Andrew was thinking as he tucked the blankets around Matthew. His effect on the boy had been immediate and dramatic. Andrew had never seen Matthew so peaceful. Strange that such a firebrand, himself so quarrelsome and restless, should be able to bring about peace in others. He remembered when Collen had been Father Abbot at the monastery. How they had loved and hated him. How he had upset their quiet routines and demanded more of them spiritually than they were capable of giving. More than once there had been angry murmuring amongst themselves. At last there had been a confrontation at the time when there were visiting bishops and abbots from other monasteries. Collen had lost his temper (as he frequently did) and accused them all, including the visiting dignatories, of being hypocrites . . . 'whited sepulchres' were his exact words . . . and had stormed out, never to be seen again until Lukas had found him living as a hermit deep in the forest at the base of the Tor.

None of the Brothers had liked to admit it, but many of them had missed the man. During his brief rule they had often been exasperated when his teaching had left them disturbed and confused: yet it always had had a grand 'lift' to it. He used words that made them look in a fresh way at what they had taken for granted. Andrew remembered the feeling of real excitement he had had that God was immediately and absolutely present in the chapel when Father Collen was roaring out his magnificent, poetic prayers . . . each one different, each one appropriate to the moment. But the administration of the monastery had irked him. It was really no surprise that his impatience got the better of him in the end.

Within a day and night Lukas himself was admitted to the infirmary. It was clear that he was ill. In spite of the care he received he grew steadily paler and thinner, the rings under his eyes darker. He dreaded the nights, refusing to sleep lest he should dream strange dreams again. He tried to pray to the archangel Mik-hael, who was supposed to give protection against demons, but found his mind wandering. Once or twice Matthew tried to raise the subject of the mysterious happenings, but Lukas refused to talk about them again. It was as though he had decided that if he didn't mention them, they would disappear from his mind. Matthew understood. He too had persuaded himself that the terrible feelings of suffering and guilt he had experienced when Lukas had mentioned 'that name' (Matthew dared not give it form even in thought) had been 'just' imagination.

When Lukas had been in bed a week and showed no sign of recovery, Brother Collen was called in to see him.

'How long do you intend to hide yourself away?' he asked brusquely as soon as he saw the young man lying curled in a great homespun blanket, only the top of his brown head and his brown eyes showing.

Lukas turned his face to the wall and his back to the hermit.

'Get up,' Collen commanded. 'This is no way to behave.'

'I'm ill,' Lukas complained in a faint voice.

'Nonsense,' was the reply. 'You are afraid.'

Lukas turned and looked up at him.

'Would you not be afraid?' he asked.

'I would,' Collen said. 'But I would also be curious.'

Lukas sighed and sat up, throwing his long legs over the edge of the bed. Collen noticed that he had lost weight, but that his eyes were clearer than they had been when he first entered the room.

'You are on the brink of understanding so much,' Collen said. 'You cannot give up now.'

'I cannot look at anything the way I used to,' Lukas said sadly. 'Everything seems different.' It disturbed him that appearances were so deceptive and that he no longer knew who he was.

Collen watched him closely.

'I cannot stay here,' Lukas said at last. 'I have to get away.'

'You will never be free unless you face what is before you now,' Collen warned.

'I know. But I cannot stay at the monastery. I cannot take my vows. I cannot live this life.'

Collen was silent for a long while.

'If you come with me I will put you to work,' he said at last.

'I will work.' Lukas' face showed the relief he felt.

'I will not help you to escape.'

54

'I know.'

'Come then,' said Collen gruffly and turned to leave.

But the Abbot was at that moment entering the room.

'What is this?' he said coldly, staring at the young man about to leave with the hermit.

Collen gave Lukas a quick wry look, bowed briefly and somewhat mockingly to the Abbot and walked straight past him and out of the door.

For a moment his fear of the man made him hesitate, and then Lukas knew that if he did not make his stand now he never would. He raised his chin and looked the Abbot straight in the eyes.

'Father, I have not yet taken my vows and I do not intend to. I am grateful for the care you have given me, but I know that this is not my vocation and I will be a burden to you no longer.'

The Abbot's face went red. He had never liked Lukas but he would have preferred to turn him out of the monastery himself than have the young man insolently rejecting it in this way.

'You have been trouble ever since you were brought here,' he snapped. 'You have rejected the Lord and the Lord has rejected you.'

These were terrible words to hear and Lukas almost lost his nerve. If the Lord had rejected him – where was there to go in the whole world that would be safe? But then he remembered Collen and knew that the Lord rejected no one – and that there was another way to accept the Lord than by following rules and regulations and obeying an unjust man.

He bowed his head gravely. In his heart he was bowing to the Lord, but the Abbot thought he was bowing to him.

'You will serve out your time in humility and repentance,' he said sternly, 'and if I decide you are truly not for the Lord's work I will release you on the day set aside for your vows.'

'No,' Lukas said with sudden boldness. 'Reverend Father Abbot, I am leaving today.' With that he strode past the man and out of the door.

In the corridor he tried not to run or look back over his shoulder. His heart was pounding uncomfortably in his chest. As he passed the door of the dormitory in which he had spent so many nights, he glanced in. There he saw Brother Collen kneeling beside Matthew who was lying on his bed. His hand rested just above his chest. The room was very quiet, quieter than a room would be with just the absence of sound. It was as though they were suspended in time somehow and Lukas was watching the man on his knees, the monk standing beside him, and the boy on the bed as though they were all part of a distant scene.

No one said anything. Nothing appeared to be happening. There was an atmosphere of beautiful, restful peace. Brother Collen himself had subtly changed. Lukas would have found it difficult to describe it to someone who had not witnessed it. Collen seemed to be listening to someone that the rest of them could not see or hear.

At last he stood up and Matthew opened his eyes and looked up at him. There was even colour in his cheeks at last and he was smiling.

Collen stood up slowly, looking down on the young boy with infinite tenderness, and then he made the sign of the cross over him. The monk standing beside them said something to Brother Collen, he replied and then turned to go.

Together Lukas and Collen walked away, neither speaking . . .

GWYNN AP NUDD, Lord of Annwn, stood upon the summit of the Tor and gazed hawk-eyed upon the lovely scene of forest, water and reeds that lay below him in every direction. Water birds were winging home.

The sky above him was darkening into night but he did not see it wheel and turn as Lukas had, nor feel the earth moving in harmony with it.

Gwynn's expression was grim.

The ancient days were almost gone. He, one of the mighty Lords of the Underworld, leader of the Wild Hunt, most feared Gatherer of Souls, had been pushed aside by the new religion as though he were some sort of outgrown toy. He would show those monks with their perpetual choir! Their prayers robbed him of his glory, stole his subjects, confined his restless heart.

It had begun with Arthur, god-King of the ancient days. Gwynn had chosen to ride with Arthur as Prince and subject, though as son of Nudd the Silver Hand he himself was rightfully an equal. The early days had been magnificent. No moon had run its cycle without a challenge and an adventure that would have filled a poet's heart with joy. Great deeds were done as frequently as man drew breath. How he had enjoyed the fellowship, the battles, the chase, the quest! Arthur himself had ridden with Gwynn's hounds across the sky and thought nothing of hunting a soul or two in those days. When Arthur was in need he had asked Gwynn for help. He had given his assistance without hesitation when the Giant Ysbadden had demanded that Arthur's young cousin, Culhwch, perform impossible feats to win his daughter Olwen. And then when Gwynn had wanted a woman of his own and had taken one, holding her by fair conquest, Arthur had turned against him.

Gwythyr! That was the name he sought. His rival. Gwynn's face twisted. He had thought he had out-witted him, yet here he was in the deceptive form of a young monk pretending not to know who he was.

Gwynn had first seen the woman Creiddylad, serving the wine to her father's guests in the great hall of her father's house. She had passed from guest to guest with the grace of summer breeze through corn. He had watched her bend and turn, swinging the heavy jar with ease, not spilling a drop, her golden hair loosely flowing from a fillet of gold around her brow, her cheeks flushed with good health, her lips smiling, honouring each guest with name and compliment as she filled each silver chalice. He remembered it had seemed an age before she reached him and when she did he took hold of her left arm as she poured with her right, gazing into her eyes, his own dark with unmistakable desire. The ready smile she had been so free to give before faded, and a shadow passed over her sunny face as cloud over flowering field.

'Sir?' she asked quietly, looking down at her arm where his hard hand was clasped so tight and painfully.

He said her name softly, almost under his breath, but didn't release her arm.

'Sir!' she said again, this time with an edge of annoyance in her voice.

Slowly he loosened his grip, and she slipped away from him. But his eyes never let her go and time and again he called for his goblet to be refilled. Each time she came to him reluctantly but bound by the rules of hospitality not to refuse him. Each time her eyes were lowered and no matter how hard he tried to make her raise them, she would not. He didn't touch her again physically, but each time she stood before him she felt his touch upon her.

After that night he didn't ride away as he had intended but lingered at her father's court, boasting with the rest of the young warriors about their battle deeds, listening to bardic tales, feasting and drinking. Creiddylad tried to avoid him, but could not. She was always polite, but never warm.

He noticed that although she hurried from him, she lingered always with another young man, Gwythyr, son of Greidyawl. He noticed too that she did not avoid his eyes as she had done his own. He noticed that even when they were on opposite sides of the room, their eyes made contact.

The time of the Spring Festival approached. The warriors prepared to leave the smokey hall. With the heroic sagas still ringing in their ears they were impatient to set off on adventures of their own. But first there was to be the ceremony to ensure the burgeoning of the earth. Creiddylad was chosen to represent the Virgin Earth; Gwythyr to provide the quickening seed of the Sun.

Smouldering with resentment, Gwynn watched the preparations. He had lived as ordinary man long enough. He was tired of the game. He would use his ancient powers to take the woman he desired. He made sure Gwythyr received false messagess and left the place of preparation, and then he took on the form of Gwythyr himself, so skilfully that no one noticed the difference. No one but Creiddylad.

As he took his place in the procession, she turned to look at him. Their eyes met, and she knew at once that it was he.

She cried out and refused to go ahead with the ceremony. No matter how her father scolded and cajoled she would not take a step towards the sacred hill while he was present. So perfect was his disguise the others thought she had gone mad and tried to force her to accept him – but her bitterness against him was so intense he soon became angry and, in his anger, lost control of the spell that held him in the form of Gwythyr.

Astonished, his companions saw his face distort with rage in a way they had never seen Gwythyr's – his eyes darkened; his nose leng-thened; his very height changed. At last revealed – a fierce and violent man, thwarted and frustrated.

The last he saw of Creiddylad that day was as she was being ushered off weeping by her women friends, while he, mighty lord, was driven from the community like some common criminal.

So they held their pretty ceremony without him and he could do nothing but grind his teeth in anger as he thought of Gwythyr entering that perfect body.

For some time he sulked, confining himself to his own realms, restless, bitter, frustrated. He was no longer content to be whom he was. He was no longer satisfied with the bodiless spirit-world. He yearned for the touch of flesh, the excitement and rough pleasures of the human world.

On the night before the wedding of Creiddylad and Gwythyr, a herd boy attending the birth of a calf looked up in alarm as a dark wind sprang from nowhere and rushed howling through the forest, snapping great branches as though they were twigs, ripping up trees that had held firmly to the earth for centuries. Shutters were fastened hastily in the great house of Creiddylad's father, but the gate had been left open for the arrival of guests and through it rode Gwynn ap Nudd on his black charger, his hounds yelping and yapping around him, his warriors beside him.

Creiddylad was seized and abducted.

Gwynn could still hear the curses of her father ringing in his ears and Gwythyr's name shouted as messengers rode off to fetch him to her rescue.

He could have taken her straight back to his own realm there and then, and there they would never have found her, had he not wanted to make love to her as man to woman.

He rode until he deemed he was out of reach and then made camp. Dishevelled and angry, Creiddylad was released from his iron grasp and tumbled on the ground. She was up at once, spitting defiance. She tried to run, but there was nowhere to go in the depth of the night, and too many men to bring her back. She straightened her clothes and drew as near to the fire as she could. When she was offered food and drink she flung it away. When he reached for her she went limp and he could have no pleasure of her.

At dawn his watchers brought him news that Gwythyr and his men were riding through the gorge. He bound her to a tree and thundered off with his men. Then followed the battle in the narrow valley and Gwythyr's men were cut to pieces. Those that were not killed were taken prisoner. Only Gwythyr himself survived, broken, defeated, helpless, limping back to Creiddylad's father – shamed. Gwynn had deliberately avoided him, wanting him to live and suffer for his men.

Among the prisoners Gwynn took was Kyledyr, Gwythyr's greatest friend, and Nwython, Kyledyr's father.

Gwynn did not tell Creiddylad that Gwythyr had survived; she assumed him dead. When Gwynn came to her again the hate in her eyes burned so strong even he felt disinclined to touch her.

'In time,' he thought, 'in time . . .'

And he turned his attention to punishing his hated rival who still held the love of the woman he desired.

He took Nwython, Kyledyr's father, and cut out his heart. He then tricked Kyledyr into eating it. When the young man learned what he had done, and Gwynn did not waste much time in telling him, he went mad with horror and guilt. Gwynn then sent him back to Gwythyr a gibbering idiot, his hair matted, his eyes wild, his mouth dribbling blood as he constantly bit his own tongue. A spy took the story straight to Arthur and suddenly for the second time, he, a Lord of Annwn, was reviled and disgraced. Arthur rode in with a vast company of men, slew Gwynn's followers and released the prisoners. He decreed that because Gwynn had won the girl in battle she could not be given back to the loser. Yet neither could Gwynn, the victor, be allowed to keep her. The doom Arthur pronounced was that she might belong to neither.

Creiddylad was escorted back to her father's house, and there she was to remain.

Gwythyr had ridden away, honouring the judgement, and soon such noble deeds were reported of him that Gwynn feared Arthur might change his mind and give Creiddylad to him after all. It was said that one day, riding in the mountains, Gwythyr had come upon a brush fire and would have ridden on had he not heard crying and sobbing coming from a mound of earth. He realized that a million ants were trapped and being roasted in the fire. He dismounted at once and moved among the flames regardless of his own danger, slicing at the anthill with his sword and lifting it free of the fire.

Gwynn, on the other hand, would not accept the judgement, and each year as the sap began to flow again in the trees of the forest he rode in through the great gate of her father's house and demanded that she come away with him.

Each year at the same time, remembering the brief flowering of their love, Gwythyr returned to the hill that overlooked her father's house and gazed with longing from afar at the windows of her chamber.

Each year Gwynn assailed her, and each year Gwythyr defended her. Tears fell from Creiddylad's eyes as frequently as the Spring rains that brought the earth into bloom.

One day Gwynn rode in on the winter storms and seized Creiddylad before the alarm could be sounded. He left the human world and returned with her to his own realm.

But still she defied him: a prisoner, not a consort; always an enemy, never a wife.

As the centuries went by and he stood upon the Tor looking out upon the world, he seethed with dissatisfaction. The boats that had ferried souls to him were now empty more often than not. The Christians with their god were drawing the human race from him and taking them to a kingdom of their own. He brooded on the power he had lost and on the power he longed to have. The world of men had changed over the centuries. Well, he had changed too! He had not been idle while the monks had been singing their songs. He had been planning to take the world from them and now he was almost ready to do so. Their god said that with faith one could move mountains. He believed that he could alter the course of the universe.

He thought of the grey figure in the cavern, old beyond belief, weary of life, but living it still because he had willed that she should. His victory would be nothing if she did not witness it.

But one more thing he needed, and then he would be capable of destroying the old order and creating his own without himself being destroyed.

Gwynn's eyes were harsh and brooding as he stared over the dark landscape. The sun had been setting when he first reached the summit. The last faint light over the western horizon now faded and he was a dark man standing in darkness.

He looked at the stars malevolently. He was sure the key he needed lay there in those vast stellar patterns.

On earth he could change any structure at will. He could make clouds. He could lash the earth with storm and hail. But the key that made the whole function as a Whole always eluded him. He could change one thing but, in doing so, he disturbed something else, which then reacted in such a way as to make his first achievement at best null and void, at worst dangerous and destructive. The secret that kept everything in balance and harmony was still a mystery. He knew that if he made his final challenge, his supreme effort to change the universe so that all would be subject to him, without achieving this balance, he would destroy it, not change it.

He came to believe that the stars held the key to the mystery.

The ancients had studied the stars and had seen that they affected all that happened upon the earth.

If he, Gwynn, could bend the motion of the stars to his own will, change the ancient configurations of the Zodiac and take the threads of its influence into his own hands, he could pull the universe to follow him and leave the invisible god, the disembodied god, the so-called source of love and harmony, helpless and defeated.

He drew himself up to his full height ready for the night's work. But he found he could not concentrate. The return of Gwythyr at this precise time could not have been an accident. He had hidden Creiddylad well and her lover had not been able to find her before. Now, at this moment when he was ready at last to make his final bid for ultimate power and he could not afford distractions, Gwythyr, in the body of Lukas, had tracked him down. Why?

With Gwythyr's presence on the Tor and the encouragement it would give that meddling monk Collen and Creiddylad herself, he could not afford to wait longer. Tonight must be the night.

He raised his arms above his head, reaching into the darkness.

'Stars!' he cried, in a voice like a great wind. 'Obey me! I Gwynn-ap-Nudd, Lord of Annwn, Holder of Power, demand it!'

Above him the stars seemed to flare like fire that had been given more fuel. Brilliant and violent, they seemed to grow and throb.

He could feel the strain of his own power and he shook like the earth in the throes of an earthquake. His will was breaking . . . his mighty scheme coming to nothing. Sweat poured from him.

Caught in the blaze of unnatural heat, his heart sobbed for relief while his mind still demanded his steadfastness. He must hold!

He must hold! Any weakness now and he would be consumed!

'I know all I need to know,' he screamed. 'I will change you from the first to the last, and your influence on man will be my influence!'

His voice was like the hurricane and from the heart of fire he challenged fire. The white flame of ambition consumed him from within. The white flame of the star's heat consumed him from without.

He could not hold. Pain was in every part of him. There was no hiding place left where it could not reach.

His will had reached to the stars and he had called them to him, but, too weak to take their power upon himself, his lips had burned and blistered, his throat had closed with agony.

He fell in a heap of hurting flesh and dusky cloak upon the ground.

Above him the great figures of the Zodiac rode silently, each in the place it had always been . . .

'WILL YOU TELL me his name now?' Lukas asked Collen.

Although he remembered most of the incident with the sword and had told his friend all he knew, the name he had shouted as he drew his weapon eluded him. Memories of dreams and of incidents in his past life as Gwythyr floated together freely in his mind, almost indistinguishable. It seemed sometimes as though the air were full of drifting seeds and bubbles, and he, a blind man, in reaching up to catch the seeds, caught only the bubbles.

Collen looked troubled and thoughtful.

'Some call him Lucifer, once a great and mighty archangel of Light – now a dark and bitter shade. In his ambition he challenged the mysterious source of all Being – the unimaginable and unnamable.

He over-reached himself. He fell. He lost all that was his. He seeks now only to destroy what he can no longer have.'

'Is there no way for him to regain the Light and be what he once was?'

'The way is always open. But he must choose to take it,' Collen replied soberly.

Lukas was silent.

'Some call him the King of Shadows, Gwynn ap Nudd, Lord of Annwn,' Collen continued musingly after a while, 'and fear him as god or demon left over from pagan times. Some say that he is no more than an ordinary man, deep into the study of the black arts.'

'Whom do you say he is?'

'He himself claims to be a hermit, like myself,' said Collen, still not answering directly. 'When I was Abbot . . .'

'You were the *Abbot*?' Lukas cried out.

Collen laughed at the expression on his face.

'I'm sorry! We can't all be what is expected of us. I had not the patience for it and that is an end of it.'

'But, the Lord must have called you to the office. Surely . . .'

'I couldn't hear His voice amongst all those people,' Collen said impatiently, and then, more thoughtfully. 'It is only when I'm alone that I can sometimes feel His presence. You think I am doing nothing of the Lord's work in this place and should have stayed an Abbot? I tell you a scarecrow appears to be doing nothing in a field, but without it the seed is eaten by the birds and the field is left bare and lifeless. A child playing with cakes of mud at his mother's knee appears to be doing nothing, but without learning the nature of the material world he cannot build a house against the rain. A man sitting on a mountain or in a desert seems to be doing nothing, but his spirit may be communing with angels and there may come a time when he will deliver the message they have given him to save the world.' It seemed almost as though the hermit had forgotten Lukas and was talking to himself.

The young man was silent. His thoughts swam close to the hermit's as though both were fish in a small pool. He understood, but could not have given the understanding voice.

'When I was your age,' Collen was speaking again. 'I made some terrible mistakes that almost cost me everything I had. I had not yet learned that when you raise yourself by inner prayer to a level of receptivity where angels can speak to you, you may open yourself to negative and evil influences at the same time, unless you fill the Silence, that shining, potent, waiting, centre within you, with the love of God and love of all that is good and positive.

'Now, when I go "into the Silence" I visualize my Lord Christ beside me and I walk step by step keeping within the circle of light that shines around him. Before I learned to do this I went too far, taking no counsellor, no precautions, following each hint of new experience without question. Ignoring a gentle intuitive warning I forced myself beyond what I now know to have been my natural limit of understanding, and found myself not in that realm of incredible, beautiful stillness, but in a frightening, nightmarish place, full of jostling, half-seen figures and noisy with strident voices. The worst thoughts of my undisciplined nature came back at me from the creatures: my pride in having come thus far while my companions were still saying the liturgies and apparently getting nowhere: my arrogant belief that I knew everything and could change the lives of everyone around me with this new source of power.

'It was when I suddenly realized the voices and the figures were not only part of my own imagination, but also outside me subtly leading me into their thrall, that I called a halt. I began to realize I would not have more power if I followed them, but less. The nature of God's grace is freedom to follow a guiding light: the nature of the Enemy's grace is slavery and a chain.

'It was a long time before I tried to go into the Silence again. And when I did, I was more aware of what I was doing.'

Lukas thought about the times in the apple orchard when 'the Silence' was very close. He had never had the courage to enter it completely. Did the Holy Spirit, the Counsellor, really live within his heart, present at all times, waiting to be listened to, his own inattention being the only reason he missed crucial guidance and help? If he listened, would he have the courage to follow? Would he have the wisdom to distinguish the true voice from the false?

There were many things he wanted to ask Collen – but the hermit had suddenly changed mood and sent him off to fetch firewood from the forest.

Later when Lukas returned to the hut Collen was standing at the entrance looking for him.

'What is it?' Lukas asked, standing with the bundle of twigs still upon his shoulder, sensing something wrong.

Collen rubbed his bearded chin and looked hard at him.

'What is it?' Lukas repeated.

'I am afraid we have a patient to care for,' he said, and his voice had a rough edge to it.

'A patient? Who is it?'

Collen indicated that Lukas should look for himself.

A premonition of danger held Lukas' heart as though in the grip of an icy hand, but within that hand, as though it were a butterfly trapped there and fluttering to get out, he could feel his heart stirring with curiosity and excitement.

He put the wood down and hurried to the hut, the hermit standing aside to let him pass, watching him closely as he walked towards the straw pallet. Light fell from the doorway onto the figure and Lukas felt sick to see the blistered and blackened face.

At first he did not recognize him, but as he watched him he groaned and moved, and as he did so, Lukas caught the lean hawk look beneath the broken skin.

He jumped back with horror.

Collen was close behind him and put his hand upon his shoulder.

'Softly. He is badly burned. We must help him.'

'Help this man?' Lukas thought rebelliously.

Collen caught the look in his eyes and gave his shoulder a kindly but authoritative squeeze. He nodded to the door.

'Fetch water,' he said.

'What happened?'

Brother Collen shrugged. 'He must have slipped and fallen into his cooking fire,' he said unconvincingly.

Lukas was too shocked by the appearance of the man to question further, and Collen was relieved that he did not. He did not want to tell him that he had found the man on the top of the Tor and that there was no sign of anything else, not even a blade of grass, having been burned.

Quietly he went to his rickety shelf and pulled out his box of healing salve. Together they washed him as best they could and dressed his burns. Once Lukas jumped as he caught the dark gleam of his eye through his half closed eye-lid – but the man showed no sign of recognition.

'He probably did not see me,' thought Lukas remembering how Cerdic often slept with his eyes partially open in the dormitory. At first it had terrified the rest of them until they discovered by cautious testing that he in fact could not see what was going on while he was asleep, no matter how unnerving the glint of his eyes might be.

'Are you going to heal him the way you healed Matthew?' asked Lukas. Collen pursed his lips, but did not reply.

'Are you?' persisted Lukas.

'We shall see,' Collen said, not committing himself.

Perhaps, thought Lukas, remembering what Matthew told him, perhaps the healing needed the co-operation of the patient and with the man unconscious it was not possible to do it. Or was it that the man was such a powerful sorcerer it would not be safe in some way? Certainly Collen seemed very reluctant to kneel by his bedside and pray as he had done for Matthew. It even crossed Lukas' mind that Collen did not *want* to heal the man. If he was such a force for evil as Collen seemed to believe, and Lukas felt, perhaps the hermit was considering leaving him 'pinned down' as it were, incapacitated, so that he could do no more harm. Perhaps he was even hoping that he would die.

As night drew nearer Lukas helped Collen prepare a third pallet of straw for the tiny hut, so that the man could lie undisturbed on Collen's bed.

When at last Lukas lay down he found he could not sleep, and spent most of the night anxiously watching the dark figure, half expecting him to rise up and cast some evil spell upon them. But the night passed and nothing happened.

By morning the patient was conscious and his eyes were as full of pain as those of an animal caught in a trap. Lukas offered him a drink of water.

The man looked from him to the cup and Lukas saw his tongue for a moment, feeling the blistered skin of his lips. He nodded almost imperceptibly. Lukas had to steel himself to put one arm behind his head and raise it slightly while he held the cup to his lips.

The man sipped thirstily, all the while seeking to look into his eyes. Lukas tried to concentrate on the cup and was determined he was not going to meet that gaze. Where was Collen? he thought desperately.

How could he leave him alone at such a time?

'What are you thinking?' the man asked as he finished drinking, his voice hoarse with pain.

'I am thinking, sir,' Lukas said, drawing back, 'that if you are such a great magician as people say, could you not heal yourself?'

The cracked lips moved painfully.

'Is that what people say of me . . . that I am a great magician?'

'Yes.'

'Do you believe them?'

Lukas hesitated. 'You can do some magic tricks,' he said scornfully, moving further back towards the door. The man's eyes flashed with anger, but he said nothing. Lukas went hastily out of the door and was relieved to find Collen outside, sitting on a stone, deep in thought.

'Why did you leave me alone with him?' Lukas demanded.

'I was here.'

'But I didn't know you were. I thought I was alone.'

'And yet you mocked him?'

'Did you hear?'

Collen laughed, and then looked sober. 'You should not mock him. He will not always be so ill.'

'Do we have to make him better?'

'Aye,' Brother Collen said. 'We do not always choose what is to be done.'

'Will he take long to mend?'

'Not long.'

'I've never seen anyone so badly burned.'

'Nor I. But he will mend.' Brother Collen frowned. 'You asked me yesterday if I was going to heal him as I healed Matthew?'

Lukas nodded.

'Everything is more complicated than it seems, my friend. Nothing can be looked at in isolation. I don't know if I can give you an explanation that will satisfy you.'

'Try,' Lukas said.

'Just as every human soul is unqiue in God's kingdom, so the way each one responds to what is given or to what happens is unique to itself. What worked for Matthew might well not work for you . . . or for our friend here.'

'But when you've decided what to do in this case – you will do it?'

Lukas persisted.

'Yes – but to make that decision is not easy. Something held me back yesterday. Partly my own reluctance I admit – but partly something else – caution . . . a feeling that this time there was something more required than mere physical healing . . . some way of making the healing reach much deeper into the soul perhaps. For this I was not sure that I was adequate . . .'

'And now?'

'And now I know it is not I but the Lord through me who will work the miracle. But even for this, poor vessel than I am, I need help. I think I see what I must do: but it will mean that I have to leave you for a while. Do you think that you can look after our patient while I'm away?'

Lukas looked alarmed.

'It won't be for long.'

'How long?' asked Lukas suspiciously.

'Not long,' Collen replied. 'I must trust you to do nothing for him but give him water if he asks. Obey no commands.'

'But . . .'

'I'll be as quick as I can.'

Lukas sighed and shrugged. 'I will do my best,' he said.

Brother Collen clapped him on the shoulder. 'Good,' he said and with no more than that, he left.

As Lukas stood in the clearing in front of the hut he had never felt so alone. He kept looking fearfully at the door and wishing that he had not taunted the sick man. If only he would sleep and Collen would come back before he woke! He sat down nervously on the flat stone the hermit had just vacated and thought hard about sleep, hoping that his thoughts would influence the patient, remembering how concentrating on finding the cavern had led him to it.

The hut was silent for so long he began to relax. After all, he thought, what could happen? The man was helpless.

And then he thought he heard a sound.

He held his breath, listening.

There it was again. This time he heard it more clearly and he knew that it was his own name being called. He went to the door and looked in. The man's eyes like dying coals glowed in the dim light within the hut. His own eyes were dazzled and half blind from the bright sunlight outside.

'Lukas,' the man said, and again, 'Lukas.'

Lukas moved to his side, unwillingly, but finding it difficult to hold back. He wondered if the sorcerer knew that Collen had gone off and that they were alone together.

'I want you to do something for me,' the man whispered hoarsely.

'I cannot,' Lukas said quickly, his heart pounding. 'I may not.'

'Cannot? May not?'

'I mean . . . I may give you water . . . but that is all.'

'You are alone?'

'No,' he said hastily. 'Brother Collen is outside, but he is busy.'

The man's tongue moved across his lips.

'Do you want water?' Lukas asked. He fancied the patient's dark head nodded faintly.

He brought him the cup and held his head again so that he could reach it. But this time the man did not drink. When Lukas leant over him his bandaged hand rose from his side and he seized his wrist and held it with a grip that almost broke the bone.

'You will do something for me.'

'No.'

'You *will*.'

'No!'

'If you do not I have tricks to make you dumb or blind. Which will it be?'

Lukas tugged as hard as he could to free his wrist, but it was held firm.

'You have no power. You are ill,' he said through clenched teeth, wishing that he believed it.

'Speak now,' the man said, and his eyes were terrible and cold.

Lukas shuddered. 'Let me go!' he tried to say, but he found that no sound came from his mouth. It was as though his tongue was as soft and formless as sheeps' wool caught on a thorn bush.

The King of Shadows smiled as he saw the terror in his companion's eyes. 'Help me,' he said, 'and I will release your tongue.'

'Never!' Lukas tried to say defiantly, but once again only his lips moved and no sound came from them. 'Please!' his eyes spoke for him, but the sorcerer took no pity.

70

'Must I demonstrate my power further?' he asked coldly.

Lukas shook his head.

'Will you help me now?'

Lukas shook his head again.

'You asked me if I could heal myself and I can – but there is something I must have in order to do it.' He winced with the effort of speaking, the shadow of pain deepening in his eyes. Lukas began to feel sorry for him. Perhaps . . .

'All I want you to do is to fetch me something from my house,' the man whispered. 'Something that will make me better faster than any of the herbs and ointments that your friend may use.'

This sounded harmless enough. Surely Collen would be relieved to return to find his unwelcome patient had recovered and left? Lukas forgot that the holy man was wanting to heal more than the sorcerer's blistered flesh and had gone off on some mysterious errand precisely so that he would be able to do this.

Lukas nodded.

'Good. Now follow instructions carefully and no harm will come to you. In my house, on the second shelf of the cupboard that faces you when you enter, you will find a small crane-skin pouch fastened with gold thread. Bring me that. Touch nothing else. Do you understand?'

Lukas could not leave his presence fast enough, and as he hurried through the forest he sang to celebrate the return of his voice.

In less time than he expected, he came to the clearing and the neatly built wooden house that he had once thought was so great and beautiful an edifice. He feared at first to enter, but reminded himself that he was doing the wizard a favour and surely no harm would come to him.

He stepped warily inside and found that it was not as grand as it had been the first time he had visited. He found the cupboard easily and on the second shelf he found a small crane-skin pouch tied with a gold thread. He took it in his hands and would have left at once with it, had not curiosity got the better of him. He had to see what was in the pouch.

He looked around quickly to make sure that he was alone, and then carefully undid the knot that bound it and gently teased it open. He peered in, but could not at first see what was inside.

71

Trembling slightly with the excitement of doing something that was forbidden, he put his fingers in and pulled the contents out. He was amazed. In his hand he held a lump of amber, as bright as sunlight. He turned it over and over, gazing into the depths of light within it, losing himself in the beauty of it, the mystery of it. And as he did so he began to feel, faintly at first and then more strongly, that this beautiful object was familiar to him. He had seen it before, and yet not in this life, not as Lukas.

'Where?' he whispered. 'When?' He turned it over and over, trying to remember. Faintly, like the dark smudges of trees in fog shadowy memories began to loom in his head.

He shook his head, trying to clear it. What was he remembering? A girl . . . eyes as blue as the sky looking into his . . . the amber on a leather thong around her neck . . . and he knowing that he had put it there, he, the chosen of the Sun . . . the sun's power contained in it . . . the sun's love warming her heart and sustaining her with its strength wherever she went.

With a sudden startling flash of knowledge he knew this talisman belonged to the girl in the cavern . . . it had been stolen and must be returned.

Triumphantly he returned it to its pouch, determined not to go back to the sorcerer, but to go directly to the other entrance to the tunnel in the apple orchard and take the girl's possession back to her.

He turned to shut the cupboard door and as he did so his eye fell on a pile of jewels that lay near the place where the pouch had lain, and which now suddenly flashed with light from the doorway.

He could not help but look at them before he shut the door. He had never seen such colour, such brilliance, such cold yet dazzling light.

A closer look! Closer.

He looked over his shoulder. He was alone. No one would know if he tried on the rings. His hand hovered over a ruby as big as his thumb nail set in gold. He slipped it on the middle finger of his right hand. He turned it from side to side, the light flashing and playing upon it. For a moment it looked as though there were something trapped deep inside it . . . a figure . . . but when he looked closer he saw that he'd been mistaken.

He was sorely tempted to keep it, but he knew that that would be foolish. He gripped it with his left hand to pull it off but it was a surprisingly tight fit.

He gave another tug . . . and another. With dawning horror he realized that he could not pull it off.

Lukas shut the cupboard door and ran back to Collen's hut. As silently and as strangely as it had come, the memory of the girl whose talisman he carried, left him and he thought no more about her.

Half way back Lukas had to cross a stream, a small flow of bright water over mossy rocks. After stopping for a moment for a drink he tried again to prize the ring off by holding his hand under water and pulling at it, thinking that it might slide off more easily if the finger were wet. But it would not move and Lukas was startled to see that the clear crystal water seemed to be taking on the deep red hue of the gem. He withdrew his hand hastily, but the stream stayed red. It reminded him of blood and he ran away from it as fast as he could, pulling and tugging at the ring as he went.

Gwynn was propped up on his elbow when Lukas reached the hut, his eyes on the door. The young man stood at the entrance and could not bring himself to enter for a moment. He gave the ring one last desperate tug, but he knew he could hide nothing from those dark and piercing eyes.

Unwillingly he stepped forward at last and put the pouch of crane's-skin beside the wizard. Then he held out his hand to show the great ruby. The hawk eyes looked at it with satisfaction, and the thin mouth smiled.

'You may keep it as a gift for your pains in fetching me what I needed,' he said.

'I do not want it,' Lukas quickly replied. 'I only meant to try it on and then I could not remove it.'

'What? Refuse a ring that would pay a king's ransom?'

Lukas looked at the ring. He had not thought beyond leaving the monastery. The ring would buy him lands enough to be a great lord. Gwynn watched him closely. Lukas could feel his eyes boring into him. He lowered his head in an attempt to escape the disturbing power of that gaze.

'I do not want it,' he repeated firmly.

'I could teach you to use it,' the sorcerer said. 'It is no ordinary ring.'

In spite of his better judgement Lukas wanted to hear more. He fingered the great stone with his left hand, watching how it flashed and sparked. It had turned a stream red. What more could it do?

He looked up and, although his mouth still shaped the word 'no', Gwynn could see from the expression of his eyes that he was eager to accept. 'Ha!' he thought. 'I have you now!' Confident in that, he now turned his attention to the pouch Lukas had brought. With shaking hands he fumbled with the gold thread, drawing it tighter rather than releasing it.

Lukas reached out to help him. He undid the thread and took out the piece of amber. How was he to know that Gwynn could not have reached the talisman, if another hand, not tainted as his had been, had not released it for him? The man smiled darkly as Lukas handed it to him, and then clutched it fiercely to his breast.

'Now leave me. I have work to do,' he said sharply. Obediently Lukas left, and sat on the flat stone outside, turning his new ring round and round in the sunlight. He fancied he saw a small dark figure deep inside the stone, but it was gone once more before he could be sure. He turned it in every direction trying to find the figure, but finally he decided he had imagined it.

The sorcerer called his name and Lukas at once rushed to the door. He found him standing tall in the middle of the hut, his skin whole and clean again, his complexion as sallow as usual, but with a healthy glow. The amber talisman was back in its pouch and strung from his belt.

Lukas was amazed.

'You see you have helped me to health quicker than your bungling friend.'

Lukas winced at the sneering tone applied to Collen, but he said nothing to defend him.

'Come, we will go now.'

'We?' Lukas asked, startled.

'Yes. You want to learn the magic of the ring,' Gwynn said. 'Come with me and I will teach you.'

Lukas looked uncomfortable. 'I am not sure,' he said. He pulled hard at the ring again.

'Hesitations? Second thoughts?'

'Yes.'

'Let me show you a sample of what I can do and maybe that will settle your mind.'

Gwynn pointed at the table. His finger was taut and stiff and Lukas could see the intense concentration in the man's gaze. Astonished, Lukas then saw that the table was no longer a table but a black cooking pot with three legs.

Gwynn smiled at his expression.

'And again,' he said, and pointed at a stool Lukas had sat on many times. It crawled away on scaly legs. There was no mistaking the astonishment and admiration in Lukas' eyes.

'There is nothing I cannot do if I choose,' Gwynn said, and added 'nothing!' under his breath with a particular emphasis as though he were trying to convince himself. 'Such trifles are easy. Whatever you see that looks solid is not solid at all. The solidity is illusion. The reality is a dance of minute and potent energies. Re-direct their paths for them and you change their appearance and their nature.'

'But . . . but how do you do that?'

'The power of mind can do anything, my friend, anything! It houses an energy that can create universes . . .' Gwynn broke off, a dark shadow crossing his face. 'But that I will not show you yet,' he muttered.

Lukas had forgotten everything but the excitement of the new skills he was about to learn. Perhaps he might have had a thought that if he learned some of the sorcerer's tricks he would be in a better position to release the prisoner, but if he had, it was not foremost in his mind.

'Could I learn to do that?' he asked eagerly, looking at the table that was now a cooking pot.

'Certainly,' said Gwynn smoothly.

'Now?'

'No. Not now.'

'Why not?'

The King of Shadows laughed. 'Could you master in one day what I have taken centuries to learn?'

Lukas looked embarrassed. He circled the 'cooking pot' curiously, wondering if it were just illusion or if a real change had taken place. Gwynn watched him amused.

'Touch it,' he said.

Lukas tentatively put out his hand. It felt real. It felt like a pot, not like a table.

75

He tapped it with his knuckle. It rang hollow.

He drew a deep breath. The man had indeed changed its entire nature.

Gwynn was watching him with satisfaction.

'Do you want something moved? I can move it,' he said, enjoying his pupil's growing admiration. He pointed his finger at the loaf of bread that was now lying on the floor, and it rose and flew towards the door.

Lukas gasped. Suddenly the room was full of moving objects.

Gwynn laughed. 'You could learn to do all that,' he said smoothly.

'Could I?' The eagerness in his heart made the triumph of the dark lord easy. He nodded.

'Come,' he said again, gathering his cloak about him. Lukas turned blindly to follow him.

He was still in the doorway, but Gwynn was outside preparing to stride off, when Collen suddenly arrived. He had been hurrying and he was out of breath, his hair more like untidy straw than ever. As he saw Gwynn with Lukas so meekly following him, he was filled with rage and his eyes sparked angrily.

'Lukas!' he shouted, and Lukas had never heard his voice so strong and fierce. He halted in confusion, looking from one to the other, no longer sure what to do.

'He is mine,' Gwynn said coldly. 'Come,' he commanded Lukas.

Lukas took a step forward.

Collen stepped between the two. He looked like a fierce fighting cock, all his feathers ruffled.

'Out of our way old meddler, or you will pay for it!'

'Let him go or *you* will pay for it,' snapped the hermit. Gwynn laughed. The noise was huge and hollow. The whole forest seemed to shudder at it.

Lukas saw Collen flex his muscles, and, fearing for his friend, he stepped forward and took him by the arm.

'He has not captured me Brother Collen,' he said soothingly. 'I'm going of my own free will. I want to learn something that may be useful to us,' he added in a whisper.

'Your own free will?' the hermit snorted. 'If it is your own free will, tell the man you will stay with me now and follow him later to learn this "art" of his!'

'Now,' Gwynn snapped. 'Or not at all.'

'Will you jump at his command, or will you stand your ground and prove that you have a will of your own?'

Lukas looked from one to the other.

'You see I have this ring,' he said at last to Collen. 'He has given it to me as a gift and I want to learn how to use it.'

'What ring?' Collen asked sharply, looking at his finger.

'This one,' Lukas held up the ruby.

'I see no ring. There is no ring there!'

Lukas stared as the ruby gleamed on his finger.

'It is illusion. He has bewitched you! There *is no ring*!'

Lukas stared at the ring again. Within the ruby . . . deep . . . deep within its depths he saw the shadow of a figure once again. He looked more closely. It was himself.

'O God,' he whispered.

'Come,' Gwynn cried. 'Do you want to learn my trade or not?'

'No,' Lukas said brokenly, in an agony of regret. He wanted to, but he knew he did not dare. He had seen the figure of himself within the gem in chains like the woman in the cavern.

'Then come and be my slave!' Gwynn screamed and lifted his finger to Lukas.

'No!' Collen shouted, and with surprising energy for such an old man, leapt upon the sorcerer, knocking him down into the dust before the deadly pointing finger could reach its mark.

'Run!' he roared at Lukas and, such was the power of command in his voice, Lukas, without thinking, ran . . .

He had not gone far however when he realized the enormity of what he had been about to do. Sorcery changed things according to the whim or will of the sorcerer – everything from cooking pots to living beings. Lukas thought about the prayers he had said daily since he could first talk – 'Thy will be done on earth as it is in heaven'. At first the words had been no more than sounds he uttered because it was expected. Then when he understood them a little better he had resented them. He did not want to obey the will of some stranger. He wanted his own will to be supreme. But now, running through the forest, he realized that if his own will were supreme then so would the will of every other individual and the ensuing chaos would be disastrous. 'Thy will be

77

done' took on new meaning. He no longer thought of God as a kind of arrogant Abbot imposing his rules and regulations arbitrarily on the world but as the source of a beautiful and satisfying creation, a living pattern of infinite variety, that had a meaning and a purpose that would be harmed by the meddling of uninformed and petty wills. He knew that much as we try to ignore it and deny it, we are capable of seeing something of that meaning and purpose, and when we do, and work in harmony with it, we find our only true joy. He was ashamed that he had left Collen in danger and run to save himself. He turned at once and retraced his steps.

He found Gwynn nowhere in sight and Collen lying on the ground as though dead.

'Holy Mother!' whispered Lukas, kneeling beside him and taking him in his arms. His weight was a dead weight, but his eyes were the eyes of a living man. Summoning all his strength he lifted the heavy body and dragged it back to the hut. What a fool he had been! What a fool!

Collen was looking at him, trying to tell him something.

'What? . . . What?' He leaned as close as he could to the ashen lips, but no sound came from them.

Desperately Lukas looked into his eyes and tried to read their message. But he could not.

In despair he sat on the floor, put his head upon his knees and tried to think. His guide and mentor was silenced: he had only himself to rely on. This thought sobered him and he pulled himself together. What should he do? What? In his mind he searched everything that had recently happened and he saw again the scene between him and Gwynn, and examined it in every detail. He remembered how the sorcerer had tried to open the pouch but had failed. At the time he had thought that it was because his hands were so damaged by the fire, and he had hastened to help him. But now – now he suddenly knew the significance of that failure: and he remembered, he *knew*, in that instant that the amber had once been his before he had given it as a gift to the one he loved. The secret magic of the talisman lay not only in itself, but in the spiritual energy of the one who possessed it.

'How did it heal the sorcerer then?' Lukas puzzled. The answer came to him with startling clarity: 'Because *I* believed it would work. Because *I* lent him *my* strength.' In that moment it did not seem strange to Lukas that he had mysterious powers bound up with an ancient talisman. It did not seem strange to him that he, Lukas, existed on many levels of time and space simultaneously; that the mysteries of his past were even now present and working through him without his conscious knowledge. He realized that we do not cease to live in the Spirit Realms because we live on earth. We may forget and need reminding from time to time just how complex and magnificent being human is, but we never lose our true capacities no matter how far we drift away into carelessness and ignorance. They are there for us to claim when we have made ourselves aware of them.

He leant over Collen.

'Can you hear me?' he asked, speaking clearly and loudly, knowing now what he must do. Collen could not nod his head, but his eyes acknowledged the question. 'I brought a pouch of crane-skin from his house and in it there was a piece of amber, a talisman, that used to belong to me. After he held it, his skin healed. I am going to fetch it now for you.'

Alarm showed in Brother Collen's eyes.

'I know,' Lukas said soberly, 'it will be dangerous. But it has to be done. I see many things clearly now that I could not see before. When you are better we will take it to the prisoner in the cavern. It is hers.' He believed at that moment it would give her the strength to free herself and to reclaim her youthful form. 'But first, I must try and undo the harm that I have done you.'

Collen's eyes looked into his, desperately trying to warn him.

'If I fail we cannot be worse off than we are,' Lukas said, and rose to leave.

But in fact many things could be worse. Collen watched him go, powerless to stop him.

12

CREIDDYLAD WAITED IN *the dark cavern and time meant nothing to her. She had long ceased to look for release from the kind of non-life, non-death, in which she was encased. Twenty years or sixty, twenty centuries or sixty millennia, might have gone by, she did not know. The one small flame of hope that burned in her heart and prevented her losing her mind, was that Gwynn ap Nudd could not, in the long run, win. However much he thought he could alter the design of existence, what he would achieve would be no more than one small aberration, soon absorbed into the whole. And she, however much the darkness she was in might seem endless, knew that it yet might be no more than a small black fleck in the whole gigantic and magnificent weave.*

But there was a cold shade that lurked beside this tiny flame. If it was known by the great Shining Ones of the upper realms that she was here suffering what she was suffering, why did they not come to her rescue?

She knew Gwynn had learnt the art of changing matter to his will. She knew he had stopped death in her and so prevented her life, her rebirth and her growth towards the light. Somehow he had closed her off from the great spirits she used to communicate with so freely.

Time and again this thought had troubled her.

Did they know? How could they not know?

She tried with all her inner strength to reach the Silence where she could hear their voices, but Gwynn had taken all her strength. Her mind floundered like a butterfly in mud, and could not take wing.

'I must not feel pain, nor fear,' she told herself over and over again. 'I must wait and rest. Strength will return with rest, surely. Surely they will come to me. Surely they will send Gwythyr to me.'

But time came and time went, and no strength returned to her crippled spirit, no message came from the great Realms of Light.

She saw only the King of Shadows, and then only for him to mock her misery.

It was hard for her to keep despair at bay: hard to keep her faith alive.

And then one day she had seen the young man . . .

At first she had not recognized him. She had seen him only as a faint hope, a stranger passing by who had seen her plight. But then when he drew his sword she saw that the great Spirits of the Realms of Light had not forgotten her. Gwythyr, for whom her heart cried day and night, her chosen one, her lover, had found her.

Now she waited for deliverance with hope, praying that the years had taught Gwythyr cunning to match his love. It was cunning and ruthlessness that had given Gwynn the edge before. She prayed that her love would not be tricked again . . . prayed that he had learned the wisdom and fortitude he would need for the task.

AFTER COLLEN HAD used his healing powers on Matthew for the second time the boy slept for nearly twenty-four hours, waking at last clear-eyed and full of energy. The first thing he did was to go to the chapel and offer up a heart-felt prayer of thanks, and then he accosted Brother Peter and pleaded to be allowed to go to Lukas. The monk looked at the thin figure before him, the pinched face, the hollow chest, the shoulder bones almost poking through the homespun tunic.

'What you need is some good wholesome food inside you,' he said. 'You'll be going nowhere until I'm sure that you have been well fed.'

'Does that mean I can go?'

'After you've eaten . . . then we shall see.'

Matthew's face broke into smiles. Brother Peter smiled back. It was impossible not to. In spite of a childhood that had been an almost continual illness, Matthew had a way of smiling that made you feel the world was the most wonderful place to be in and that you and he were sharing the secret of just how narrowly you might have missed being part of it.

Brother Peter took Matthew to the kitchen and pulled out a stool with three long spindly legs. He set before him a platter full of newly baked rye bread, a beaker of creamy milk and some good red apples, the last left in the storage barrel from the previous season's harvest. He watched with satisfaction as Matthew ate hungrily.

'I get the feeling,' he said after a while, 'that you and Lukas have some kind of secret between you.'

Matthew looked at him with bright eyes, and then took a huge bite of the bread. It was clear that he did not intend to reply.

'What did you talk about when you were together?'

Matthew frowned. 'All kinds of things,' he said.

'What things?'

'Dreams and things.'

'Tell me about the bad dream that made both of you ill.'

Matthew was silent. All that Lukas had told him had been in confidence and nothing on earth would make him betray it. He hoped that Brother Peter would not press him because he loved Brother Peter as a father, but Lukas was his liege lord and friend and he had vowed . . .

Matthew frowned. '*Liege lord*?' he thought. 'Why did I think that?'

'It may help us to help both of you if we know what is going on,' gently insisted Brother Peter.

Matthew had stopped chewing now and was sitting on the high stool, crumbling the remaining bread abstractedly on the platter. It looked as though his thoughts were far away . . . searching . . .

Brother Peter watched him, and waited. Suddenly Matthew wriggled off the stool.

'I must go,' he said with a worried look. 'He needs me. He is in trouble . . .' He ran to the door.

'Stop,' cried Brother Peter. 'Matthew . . . stop! I'll come with you . . .'

But in spite of his frailty Matthew was already out of the door and away before Brother Peter could get his great bulk across the room.

Cerdic and a few boys were digging in the herb garden as Matthew rushed past. They stopped what they were doing and looked after him in amazement.

'Hey! Chicken-bone!' yelled Cerdic. 'What's the hurry?' But

Matthew neither saw nor heard him.

Brother Peter now appeared at the door and called after him.

'I'll fetch him back for you Brother,' shouted Cerdic excitedly, flinging down the hoe and starting to run.

Brother Peter remembered too late that Cerdic had a long history of bullying and that he had a particular dislike of Matthew.

Cerdic had leapt over the low stone wall bordering the little garden and was running after Matthew with long strides.

'Come back! Come back!' called Brother Peter helplessly. 'Cerdic leave him alone! It's all right. I don't want him back!' But even if he heard Cerdic took no notice. The excitement of the hunt was on and his quarry was proving to be surprisingly fleet of foot.

The other boys stared after them, the small figure of Matthew disappearing round the corner of the refectory, Cerdic's lanky figure gaining on him, and a long way behind them both, Brother Peter panting and calling.

Matthew was frantic. He had heard Cerdic's shout and he knew that it was he who was pursuing him. He knew also that even if he were in perfect health he would not be able to outrun Cerdic. Already his chest was beginning to ache with the effort. He really feared Cerdic, and always had. If only Lukas could rescue him now as he almost always had before! But Lukas himself was in trouble. He felt it. He knew it. He looked round himself for somewhere to hide and saw the huge wooden water butt that stood close against the refectory wall to catch the rain water. There was just room for someone as thin as himself to squeeze behind it. Splinters dug into his flesh as he pushed himself in, but he hardly noticed, green slime and moss squelched underfoot where years of dripping had turned the earth to a morass. He could see that the wood was rotten and prayed that it would not give way while he was there to drown him just when he had been given a new lease of life.

Cerdic rushed past. He did not cast a glance at the water butt or the frightened creature hiding behind it, but pounded on around the corner of the refectory. Matthew tried to still the heaving of his chest, terrified that he would cough and give himself away. Before the hermit's second visit he would not have been able to stop himself, but now, although it needed a tremendous effort of will to breathe as Brother Collen had told him to breathe, he managed it. Perhaps one

83

day he'd be as strong as Cerdic and then . . .

But his train of thought was broken by the panting arrival of Brother Peter. He was still calling Cerdic, and Cerdic having lost sight of Matthew, doubled back to join the monk.

'He's gone to ground,' Cerdic said, 'but I'll soon flush him out.'

'I don't want you to "flush him out" Cerdic,' said Brother Peter with considerable irritation. 'I have sent him on an errand. I just wanted to . . .'

Matthew was amazed that they could not hear his heart beating. They were standing very close to him and his heart was pounding like a drum.

Cerdic looked disappointed and sullen. 'I could have run your errand for you Brother.'

'You could have, but I didn't ask you. I asked Matthew.'

Cerdic bit his lip and glowered at the man. 'You never ask me,' he muttered under his breath.

'What? What did you say?'

'I said you never send me on any interesting errands. It's just work, work and more work with me and if I stop for a moment it's punishment I get.'

'You know you're talking nonsense. You must learn to discipline that bitter, complaining tongue of yours.'

Brother Peter squared his shoulders and walked away, trying not to say something he would later regret. Try as he would he could not like Cerdic, and it was obvious the boy could sense it. He felt that they had failed with him. Cerdic had never understood what they were trying to do at the monastery. He must have a word with Father Abbot and see if Cerdic could not be sent away from the community to take his chances in the world. He was old enough and it was quite clear that he would not make a good monk. 'Whereas,' Brother Peter thought regretfully, 'Lukas had the potential to be a true warrior of the spirit, a true seeker.' Cerdic sought nothing beyond his own animal gratifications.

Matthew held his breath as Cerdic stood on a block of stone and reached into the water butt for a drink of water. He was hidden by the curve of the wood and Matthew could not see him, but he could hear the slurp of the water as Cerdic scooped it out and the creak of the wood as he leaned against it.

At last Cerdic left and Matthew emerged. He found that he had cramp in his muscles from the awkward position he had been forced to stay in so long and could barely walk away. He started to limp towards the orchard, remembering Lukas' tunnel. He knew that he would have no chance of finding him in the forest.

THE ABBOT PACED *his chamber. Something was threatening. He could feel change coming. He sensed the onset of disorder, of the unexpected, of the untamed. If he had his way that rebel Collen would be driven away. He was a heretic, a trouble-maker. Angrily he thought about how he had come into their infirmary and 'laid on hands' as though he were Christ himself. Who was he, a foul smelling degenerate from the woods, someone who had walked out on a calling, who had sneered and jeered at his colleagues and superiors, to call on the name of Christ? He himself had tried 'laying on of hands' on more than one occasion and had failed to bring about any kind of change in the wounded or sick person. He had put it down to the fact that the patient was sinful and unregenerate and that Christ did not want him healed. But Collen would have said that* He *was sinful and unregenerate, that he was not calling on the Name with a clear heart, that* He *was not calling at all but mouthing meaningless sounds . . . He could feel his hatred of Collen seething inside him. The muscles in his neck and shoulders tightened till they ached. His stomach rumbled and churned.*

But even behind his hatred of Collen another shadow stirred. He had always felt something lurked on that Tor, something that would not be controlled by his rules and punishments, something that pulled at that side of himself he believed to be evil – the urge to push his seed into women, to procreate, to spill out in ever increasing abandonment . . . Sometimes the iron rule of chastity was too much to bear and even to see the way nature sported in fecund pleasure in the forest on the slopes of the Tor made him uneasy. Every time he walked there he felt it. He had

85

to battle with part of himself. Safe in the monastery with every moment of the day under control he was all right. But step into the forest on that magical hill and all the old desires began to stir again. He hated Collen for having broken free and he hated the Tor for making him lust for life.

THE WAY TO Gwynn's house was not so easy to find without the wizard's help and after a few false turns Lukas knew that he was lost.

He stopped.

'I must sit down,' he told himself. 'I must think.' To go wrong now would only compound the mischief he had done and there would be no help for Collen or for any of them.

He thought about the amber talisman he was seeking, and wondered at the mystery of its power. He knew that there were holy relics in the monastery kept in precious caskets. In times of great need they were brought out and fervent prayers were said over them. He understood that the monks did this to draw on the strength of the man to whom the relic had once belonged, knowing that their own strength or purity was not enough.

Was this how the amber worked?

Lukas found that the image of the amber grew stronger in his mind the more he thought about it. He began to see it clearly with his eyes shut, almost as though it were an after-image on the inside of his lids. He kept very quiet, very still, letting the image float within his mind. Sometimes it almost faded. But it came back, and the longer he sat quiet, the steadier and stronger the image became.

'Perhaps it will help me if I allow myself to be helped,' he thought, and waited, in readiness. Soon he felt strengthened and stood up to continue his search for the sorcerer's house, this time finding his way through the forest by 'following' the image in his mind's eye.

Having in this way finally located the house, he was startled to find it guarded by two large and vicious hounds snarling at the door. He retreated to the cover of the forest, the initial feeling of elation at the success of his search, fading fast.

But then a thought struck him. What if the dogs were not there at all? What if his own fear had conjured them, or allowed the sorcerer to conjure them for him? The house had never been guarded before, and two such great hounds could not have been found in the village or anywhere nearby and trained to guard in the little time that had passed since Gwynn had left Collen paralysed.

Lukas resolved to ignore them and took a bold step forward. But then he paused. The black pot that Gwynn had conjured from the table had felt very real and very solid.

He hid behind a tree and looked at the hounds. Their teeth and the saliva that dribbled from their mouths looked very real indeed. And yet . . . and yet the ring that he had worn, that he had seen, and felt, upon his hand had not been there.

What was real and what was not, no longer seemed to have any meaning . . . or at least it seemed to have a different meaning to the one he had always accepted without question. The only thing he was sure of was that he, the person who was doing the thinking at the moment, was real, even if he was no longer exactly sure who he was.

He felt suddenly very tired.

If only he could just walk away, return to the kitchen and say to Brother Peter: 'May I come back? May I scrub pots and chop wood for you again . . . and have everything back exactly as it used to be.' But he knew that the shoot that had broken through the seed casing and was reaching for the sun could never return to the seed again. The process of life and growth had started and must be followed through to the end, before a new beginning. And that each new beginning was never exactly the same as the last.

He sighed. But then he remembered that the strengths and weaknesses of this life are not the only ones that make us what we are!

Another flash of memory came and he moved boldly forward.

'Gwynn, son of Nudd,' he called, remembering now his enemy's name. 'Give me the talisman you have stolen!'

The hounds were sharply called to heel by a stern voice from within the house, and then Gwynn himself appeared at the door.

The two stood gazing at one another for what seemed a long time, neither giving ground.

'Gwythyr, son of Greidyawl,' Gwynn said at last, coldly, harshly. 'I envied you once. But that was long ago. I defeated you once. But that too was long ago. Do you come now to challenge me knowing that I am even stronger than I was then, and that you are weaker?'

'No,' Gwythyr said, equally coldly. 'I challenge you now knowing that I have knowledge that I did not have then. Time has passed for me too and taught me many things. You will give me that talisman and I will heal the hermit Collen and release the Lady Creiddylad.'

'Never!' snarled Gwynn, lifting his arm and starting to point. But Gwythyr's hand was up before the sorcerer could direct his power. He held his own palm outwards, facing Gwynn as though to stop a beam of light. Gwynn staggered and dropped his hand, rubbing it with the other as though it was painful.

Gwythyr walked forward steadily, holding up his hand.

Gwynn took a step back, his eyes full of hate.

The hounds growled ominously, but Gwythyr ignored them.

He held in his mind's eye the image of the beautiful Creiddylad and the amber that she had worn as token that sun and earth, spirit and body, were joined in a great cosmic dance – a dance from which life flowed in ever increasing splendour.

He did not even see Gwynn as he strode towards the door, nor hear him shriek with rage. It was as though there were a great area of light within his mind within which stood the image of Creiddylad, tall and free, holding the amber above her head, and from it rays of beaded light were spreading to the far corners of the universe. He did not even notice that he had given the man a push and sent him sprawling, nor did he hear the hounds yelping as though they had been struck.

He reached into the cupboard and seized the crane-skin pouch.

As his hand touched it the brilliant image in his mind burst into a thousand fragments of light and scattered in every direction . . .

Suddenly he was Lukas once more in the sorcerer's den, holding the talisman, Gwynn's crouched figure between him and the door. In that instant Gwynn seemed to sense the change of power, and leapt towards him.

Lukas darted forward, slipped through the man's grasp and ran from the place as he had never run before, the pouch and its precious contents firmly in his hand.

'After him!' He heard the dreadful voice command, and then he heard the hounds!

Sick with fear he dodged and ran. He jumped and caught on to the overhanging branch of an oak. He struggled up to the highest branches. The hounds barked below him, hurling themselves into the air and falling back yelping when they found that they could not reach him.

But Gwynn had not given up. He lifted his hand once more and a great wind roared through the forest, bending the boughs, tearing at them, ripping the smaller trees from the earth.

Lukas clung in desperation to the stout branches of the oak, never letting go his hold upon the pouch, knowing that in spite of everything, what he held there was not in the power of the sorcerer and was his only chance of victory.

Following the wind came sheets of rain . . . thunder . . . lightning . . . Hailstones as big as pebbles beat upon his head. But soaked and bruised and terrified, he still clung to the branches and to the pouch.

And then a small ray of hope came to give him cheer. There was an advantage after all in not being able to return to the seed, not being able to undo what had been done. He had grown. He had learnt. He was no longer as ignorant as he had been when this adventure began. He would outwit Gwynn yet!

He called his name into the wind.

'Gwynn, son of Nudd,' he called. 'Lord of Winter, of Darkness and of Death!'

The raging storm ceased. Gwynn thought that he was surrendering. As he watched Lukas climb down the tree, his eyes gleamed with triumph.

'Gwynn,' Lukas said as he stood once more upon the earth. 'I will not give you this talisman. It is not yours, and I know you cannot take it.' Swiftly he pulled the thread of gold and held the amber in his hand. He raised it and held it towards Gwynn.

'Look at it . . . it is the very opposite of the power you use – it is the power of Light, the power of Love. You cannot touch it now unless someone willingly gives it to you, for when you had it, you threw it away.' He remembered how Collen had told him the man of shadows had once been an archangel of light and he himself, as Gwythyr, remembered how Gwynn had once been one of the Lords of Annwn, a mighty shining warrior riding through the clouds, gathering the souls of those who were ready for the far kingdom, for the golden lands beyond the water. He had not been a dark and evil figure then. What had changed him? What had made him greedy to take what was not his and hold it with such ruthless cruelty? What had soured and corrupted him?

Still holding the amber and using its power, he walked boldly past Gwynn and away through the forest to Collen's hut.

The sorcerer stared at him with smouldering eyes, but could do nothing.

Lukas laid the talisman on Collen's chest and folded the hermit's hands around it. Then he knelt beside him. He believed the amber to be capable of bringing about magical transformations and tried to will it, by his concentrated thought, to perform its magic on Collen. But gradually his own mind seemed to stop thinking, and a feeling of great quiet and peace took over. He felt a kind of resignation. The amber was nothing in itself, only its association with love had any relevance to them now. Love, greater than themselves – the love of harmony and order and wholeness . . .

It was at the moment that this vision took over and the thought of superficial magic faded that Collen found that he could move his fingers.

The light from the jewel pulsed and glowed, sending the warmth of the sun, ancient forests and living trees throughout his limbs.

'How beautiful,' Lukas thought. 'How beautiful!'

Collen hauled himself up, a broad smile on his face.

'Your lady must be very close to God's heart,' he said.

'You can move!' Lukas shouted in delight. 'You can talk!'

Collen laughed. 'I can also feel!' he said ruefully, as Lukas in his excitement slapped him heavily on back and shoulders.

Lukas pulled himself together and they decided the sooner they took the amber to its rightful owner, the sooner she would be able to benefit from its energies.

Collen seized the lantern and lit it, while Lukas started to pull the stones from the wall.

'What if we cannot find her?' Lukas asked anxiously.

'We will find her,' Collen said confidently. 'Just mind where you're putting those stones. I don't want to lose the use of my limbs again!'

'If I take the amber out of its pouch it might lead us to her.'

'No,' Collen said. 'I feel it should be kept covered as much as possible. We don't know what we are dealing with here. We'll find her.'

Pictures began to come to Lukas . . . Creiddylad working at her loom in her father's house, sunlight on her hair, he a young man tongue-tied before her beauty . . . Creiddylad carrying the ale jar for her father's guests, stooping to pour into his cup, her hair brushing his cheek, smiling at him with her eyes and then turning her head quickly from him so that he would not think her too bold . . . Creiddylad watched by the warrior Gwynn . . . Creiddylad chosen by the priests to play the role of the three-fold goddess of the Earth and his joy as he learned that he was to be chosen for the Sun. Then other memories not so sweet . . . longing and desire . . . fear of losing . . . rage . . . riding with his heart bursing . . . his steed sweating . . . his men around him shouting . . . How he had cried to all the gods of the earth and sky to avenge his cruel loss! But he had lost her. And he had lost his friend Kyledyr. Poor mad Kyledyr.

Dark Gwynn had won.

Then Arthur, part king, part god, had put her back in her father's house and forbidden either of them to touch her. Bitterly he had ridden away, death preferable to him than a lifetime of longing that could not be satisfied.

Years . . . was it centuries? . . . passed and the old ways changed. Arthur was no longer remembered as a god. Gwynn and he had fought savagely year after year on the appointed day, the first of May, the day Creiddylad and he had lain together as man and woman, as god and goddess . . . but neither Gwynn nor he prevailed against the other . . .

The old gods were forgotten and a new religion taught that vengeance was wrong, that forgiveness and love, even towards enemies, were right. At first he had denied this . . . but then one day . . . at last . . . the day he set the ants free from the fire . . . peace came to his heart and he decided to meet with Gwynn on the appointed day unarmed and speaking of peace. Gwynn did not keep the appointment that day. He too had decided to break through the doom of Arthur – but in a different way. He had seized Creiddylad once more and no one knew where he had taken her.

Lukas moved now through the dark tunnel with the determination of Gwythyr to find the girl he loved. He could scarcely distinguish which memories were his own as Lukas, and which came from the times long ago when he used the name and the body of a man called Gwythyr, son of Greidyawl. He could no longer distinguish between the prisoner he had seen, Creiddylad the beloved of Gwynn and Gwythyr, and the lovely life-giving goddess of the Earth . . .

Collen, who could sense the changing play of emotions in his companion, said nothing.

Gwythyr stopped at last before the stone that was marked.

He pressed it and it opened easily.

Inside the cavern their lantern illuminated the figure of an old, old crone, thin as a skeleton, grey as dust, sagging forward from her chains. As they entered she lifted her head and her eyes met those of Gwythyr. A smile spread over her face like the first light of sunrise, and with it came an ecstatic beauty that made his heart skip a beat. From that ancient shrivelled body an ageless spirit looked out.

Gwythyr ran forward and took her in his arms. He felt again the petal soft flesh, the vibrant strength of life coursing through her limbs. How many years, how many centuries had these two longed for each other? Was there not time for one long kiss?

'No time,' Collen urged. 'We must get out of here!'

Knowing that he was right, the two forced themselves to draw apart. With trembling hands Gwythyr untied the thread of gold and handed her the lovely jewel that had known the mystery of life and had conquered time.

There was a sudden explosion of light, and the chains that had bound her fell away. She was free to move. But now she was also free to die.

Gwythyr looked at the frail and aged woman before him, his heart breaking, but his love for her undiminished.

Collen touched Lukas' arm impatiently, and with the touch the burden of the present returned. It was Lukas who stood in the cavern and Lukas who remembered the King of Shadows.

'I had forgotten,' he muttered, drawing back from the grey and shaking figure.

'Take me to him,' she said. 'There is something I must do before I die.'

Lukas stood irresolute, confused.

'Come!' Collen urged. 'It has to be. He'll be up on the Tor, and there is no time to lose.'

He lifted the frail figure in his arms and ran with her to the entrance to the cavern, and then along the tunnel towards his hut. Lukas followed, almost staggering from the strain of slipping between two lives, two memories.

When they reached the place where they had taken the stones out of the hermit's wall so that they could enter the tunnel, they found that they had been fitted back, and so firmly that with all their strength, they could not be moved.

Lukas and Collen looked at each other in despair. The woman was breathing unevenly. They had put her on the ground and she was leaning against the dirty wall beside the lamp, with scarcely strength to lift her head. But in her thin and wizened hand she held the golden fire of the amber. Fearing that she might drop it Lukas moved to take it from her, but she shook her head faintly and said in a voice so thin and low it was almost impossible to distinguish the words.

'I must hold it . . . it is the only thing that is keeping me alive now.'

Lukas left her and hurried back to the wall.

'There is no way we'll break through here,' Collen said.

'There's the entrance in the apple orchard,' Lukas reminded him. He thrust the lamp into Collen's hands and lifted the frail form in his arms. He scarcely felt her weight as they ran down the passage. But then a thought struck him.

'If *he* put the stones back in the wall, he must know that we are down here.'

'Without a doubt,' agreed Collen.

'What if he has blocked off the other entrance?'

They increased their pace, chilled by the thought that they might well be trapped in this horrible place as Creiddylad had been, prisoner of such a Being, never to see the light again.

Collen was ahead and suddenly gave a joyful cry. He had found the entrance and it was not blocked. Whatever elaborate and sinister game Gwynn ap Nudd was playing with them it did not include imprisonment. It crossed Collen's mind that he wanted them to escape and had only been buying time when he had closed the exit in the hut. The orchard was much further from the Tor and from there it would take them much longer to reach him.

Lukas gave Creiddylad into the care of Collen as he climbed the pile of rocks and earth to push the make-shift lid of branches out. The lantern rested on a pile of debris. Pieces of earth fell into his face, roots dangled down like ragged curtains and touched his shoulder.

With the lid once drawn back Lukas climbed out, looking anxiously round the orchard to make sure that they were alone. Then he reached down and Collen lifted Creiddylad to him. The hermit followed, extinguished the lamp and put the lid back over the hole.

The sunlight dazzled the woman and she shut her eyes, turning her head against Lukas' shoulder.

'Could we rest awhile?' she pleaded. 'It's so long since I have seen the sunlight.'

'A while perhaps – but not more than a few moments,' conceded Collen. He himself was in need of a rest and glad that he had not been the one to ask for it.

Lukas stood beside her and looked at her. She was old, older than anyone he had ever seen. Her clothes were rags, and her skin was dusty, but she was beautiful.

Slowly she opened her eyes a crack. Shut them again. Opened them a little wider. He watched her, fascinated, trying to imagine how it must be to see the world after such a long, long time of darkness. At first she screwed up her face so that only the minimum of light could reach her and he noticed how she held the talisman tenderly up to her face, as though it were helping her to see. When at last she managed to keep her eyes fully open she slowly turned her head around gazing at everything with an expression of delight. She touched a little pad of moss that grew on a gnarled old root and stroked the fine grass beside her. She asked to be shown a snail that was crossing the path in a leisurely manner, and Lukas rushed to fetch it for her. After she had gazed at it for a long time and traced the spiral markings of its shell with a thoughtful finger, she asked for it to be set back in its place. Once on the ground again it continued in the same direction as though there had been no interruption in its quiet journey.

Collen stood up again and urged that they waste no more time. 'We must get to the Tor before it is too late,' he said.

'Too late for what?' Lukas wondered, rising from the grass, but wishing that they could have stayed there forever.

Collen helped the lovely lady to her feet.

'The time has come for us to challenge him and he is aware of it,' he said. 'Who knows what he will do.'

'What do you think he'll do?' Lukas looked at Creiddylad.

She was slow to reply.

'I don't know how much you remember,' she said at last. Lukas, who found it increasingly difficult to distinguish between his dreams, his memory and his imagination, shook his head.

'Tell us all we need to know,' he said. 'I can't trust my own memory any more.'

Collen nudged Lukas to remind him that they must be moving on and he lifted her again. She began to tell them something of the background to her long imprisonment as they walked towards the Tor. Lukas strained to remember the things that she talked about. Most vividly he remembered that day on the Tor when he made love to her, and the full moon stood beside the sun in a blue and endless sky.

She smiled and met his eyes as though she remembered too – and then a shadow crossed her face. 'Gwynn could have stayed a mighty spirit Being but he chose to manifest as man. At first, perhaps intending only to stay a short while, but leaving it too long and taking on earth-nature so effectively that in the end he was neither one thing nor the other – lost between worlds, capable of all that a great Lord of Annwn is capable, yet motivated by the greed and jealousy that comes so easily to human-nature. He wanted to take, rather than give, to dominate rather than love. He began to believe that his mind, existing in time, was superior to his spirit, existing outside time.'

'A fallen angel,' Collen muttered.

'A Being in need of help,' Creiddylad said softly.

'Surely you're not sorry for him?' gasped Lukas, almost letting her fall as he stumbled against a stone.

The woman nodded thoughtfully.

'Is it so easy to be what you should be?' she asked softly.

Lukas flushed and conceded in his heart that it was not easy. Not easy at all.

16

CERDIC HAD STARTED to return to the herb garden frustrated and angry. He felt he had been humiliated in some way. He had tried to help and his offer had been scorned. He was not fooled by Brother Peter. Matthew had been running *from* him, not on an errand *for* him. Why had he not been trusted to bring him back? Was it because of that incident the other night? It had been an accident. How was he to know that Matthew would nearly die? Besides, would it have been such a great loss if he had? Why was he, Cerdic, never trusted? Whenever there was something responsible to be done he was passed over. If he had been missing from duty half the time that weasel Lukas had been lately he would have been punished by extra duties or made to kneel on the icy flagstones of the chapel until he was stiff and sore in every limb. There had been that incident when he had been caught with one of the village girls behind the cow shed. If she hadn't screamed out he would have got away with it. He was called up before Father Abbot and made to listen to a lot of pious words about how he would be tortured in hell for the sin of lust – and after that he was punished and looked on as some kind of filth. The younger boys used always to be whining about him, but lately he had stopped all that and they held him in proper awe. He was king of the roost. He had proved himself time and again, violently and powerfully, and not one of the boys dare question him or disobey his bidding. He sometimes thought . . . and here his glowering mood lightened a little . . . he sometimes thought that even the monks were afraid of him.

The group of boys in the herb garden had stopped work and were sitting on the wall talking and laughing, looking out for Cerdic, clearly delighted that he had not caught Matthew. A wave of hot anger seemed to rise up through his body and a kind of fierce red blindness overcame him. Brother Peter had returned to the kitchen and was

96

nowhere in sight.

Cerdic picked up the hoe and turned on his heel, striding back the way he had come, his mouth in a tight angry line, determined to capture Matthew whom he blamed for what he thought of as his latest humiliation.

Matthew, unaware of all this, had reached the path that led to the orchard but had not yet put a foot on it, when he heard something behind him and turned round. Horrified, he saw Cerdic, knew what he had in mind, but knew also that this time he would not be able to escape.

Cerdic saw the fear in his eyes and raised the hoe. He brought it down on the boy's head and shoulders again and again while Matthew struggled to dodge and run. Cerdic could think of nothing but beating him to the ground as he had a ferret that had bitten him only a few weeks before.

The other boys had followed and now stared with horror as Matthew began to sob and plead for mercy, blood pouring from him. Not one of them made a move to help him, though there were many there who saw their own fate in his.

Having satisfied himself that the iron grip of fear he had always had on his minions was secure again, he held off for a moment and demanded to be told where Matthew had been intending to go and where exactly Lukas was. When Matthew did not answer he beat him again. Cerdic could see that his dogged courage was beginning to sway the sympathy of the crowd behind him and he could not afford to allow this. The blow he brought down on Matthew's head this time almost split his skull and the boy fell forward with a sickening lurching movement that drew a gasp from those watching. He hit the ground and lay horribly still.

For what seemed a long, long time the boys and Cerdic stood staring at Matthew, not wanting to believe what they saw.

Suddenly the watchers turned and ran, tumbling over each other to get away, leaving Cerdic shocked and stunned, staring at what he had done.

When the Brothers Peter, Andrew and Owen arived, running, followed by a stream of agitated boys, they found that Matthew was still lying where he had fallen, but Cerdic was nowhere in sight. The blood-stained hoe lay quite a distance away as though it had been flung there with some considerable force.

Brother Peter lifted Matthew in his arms, tears streaming down his cheeks. 'Why? Why?' he asked himself desperately. Had they not given Cerdic a place to live when he was lost and lonely? Had they not given him care, and tried to give him a sense of purpose? But he had never understood . . . never been grateful . . . always believed that everyone hated him until it had become a truth. They had tried to love him because their Lord had told them to love everyone – but Cerdic made it almost impossible. Sullen, disagreeable, cruel . . . he had been at the centre of every bit of trouble they had had in the last years. They and he were trapped in a vicious circle: the worse he behaved, the less he was loved: the less he was loved, the worse he behaved. Nothing seemed to get through to him. The monks had prayed for him: but the Lord had given them no guidance except the uncompromising command: 'love and forgive'.

COLLEN WAS NOT as young as he would have liked, and on more than one occasion on the way to the Tor he had to pause for breath. At such times Lukas lowered Creiddylad to the ground beside him, and paced restlessly around, anxiously estimating how far they still had to go.

The afternoon sunlight flickered through the new green leaves of the forest and Creiddylad looked up in wonder at the sky glittering like tiny fragments of sapphire through the intricate filigree of gold and emerald. Sometimes she stroked the earth as though it were the child she loved and had been parted from for a long time.

'It's a pity there is no more of that holy water left,' Lukas said to the hermit. 'We might have need of it.'

'Don't fret about it. I would not go to such an encounter as we expect unarmed!' and he patted his side where Lukas could just see the bulge of the pewter water bottle strung from his belt and half hidden by the folds of his clothes.

'I thought you threw the last at me?'

'There is always more in the sacred well.'

'Is that what you were fetching when you left me alone with Gwynn?'

Collen nodded.

'I thought all water was holy,' Creiddylad said, puzzled. 'It brings life and comes from God.'

'Ah,' said Collen, 'it may be so – but sometimes we need a little extra something to strengthen our confidence.'

She smiled and bowed her head in acknowledgement.

'I have my amber talisman,' she said and raised it to her lips and kissed it. As she did so her face seemed to glow and for a moment she looked young again.

'We must get on if we are to do all that has to be done,' Collen said briskly. 'Come Lukas – enough dallying!'

Lukas lifted Creiddylad, whose brief moment of youth had already passed, and the little party set off again. They took the same route that Lukas had taken that first time when he had encountered the stranger on the Tor, the path in many places overrun with thorny strands of bramble and phalanxes of nettle.

When they finally reached the first of the faintly marked earth walls that Lukas had noticed that first day, her face lit up. 'You need carry me no further,' she said and slipped to the ground.

'I think you should . . .' Collen began to say and then he stopped because he could see that she was standing now as straight and tall as a young woman.

Lukas remembered the girl with the flowering bough and the green cloak in his dream. A twig of apple buds he had given Creiddylad in the orchard was still clutched in her hand, but now it was a blaze of blossom. She looked at it, smiling, her eyes the colour of the summer sky.

Lukas rushed off the trail and broke off two more branches for Collen and himself, one of hawthorn and one of oak. The hermit took the oak without question. He knew that they were all to play their part in a strange and ancient drama and held himself in readiness. Whether he himself had been one of the original protagonists he did not know. What his role would be exactly no one could tell. But he knew, whether he liked it or not, he had become part of it and he must see it through to the end. He followed quietly as they began to climb.

Below them in the forest, though they did not know it, Cerdic ran, stumbling from one path to another, hardly aware of what he was doing, or where he was going, knowing only one thing and that was that he wanted to get as far away as he could from the pale bleeding figure of the boy he had left for dead.

At each turn of the spiral the woman seemed to grow younger until by the time that they were nearly free of the forest she was the young girl Lukas had seen in his dream. Her beauty made them gasp – but even as they gazed at her in admiration a chill shadow passed over them. They looked up – and were shocked at what they saw. A tall building towered over them that Lukas knew had not been there when he had climbed the Tor before. It bore a close resemblance to the image he had first seen of the sorcerer's house in the forest, the entrance guarded by tall columns of dark wood carved all over with sinister two-faced severed heads and weird designs of monstrous beasts and deformed men and women.

Gwynn ap Nudd himself stood before the doorway, his eyes glowing like live coals, his cloak of shadows falling at his side like the giant folded wings of a bird of prey, watching and waiting.

The man had been transformed. How could they hope to touch him now with their little bottle of well water, no matter how holy, their boughs and their piece of amber?

'He's seen us,' whispered Collen hoarsely. And as he spoke the words, they were filled with such dread that they found that they could no longer move their limbs.

They heard a voice as hollow as thunder in a cave.

'You are welcome,' the darkness from the centre spoke. 'I have prepared a feast for you.'

They stared at him, wanting to speak, but no words would come from their numb lips. Lukas remembered the time in Collen's hut when he could not speak and he felt sick with fear.

The King of Shadows raised his arm and the sound of it was like the sound of giant wings beating above them.

'Come!' he cried, and they found that they could move their limbs again but only in the direction that would bring them nearer and nearer his dread presence. Lukas looked to Collen for comfort, but he found that the hermit was looking as frightened as he was. Only Creiddylad held her head high and walked ahead as though she were choosing of her own free will to do so.

Lukas felt ashamed, and gave up all thought of fleeing.

They walked between the great columns. They entered the hall. The Lord of Annwn walked ahead of them and took his place on a huge and gleaming throne of gold. They stood before it dwarfed by the great wooden columns that held the roof up, by the huge carved wooden statues on either side of the throne, and by Gwynn himself who seemed to be larger than any man they had ever seen.

In the centre of the hall a long banquet table had been laid with the most delicious food it was possible to imagine. The dishes were of gold, the goblets of fine crystal. Lukas' mouth watered until he remembered the last time he had been faced by one of Gwynn's feasts.

Around the table on smooth, well-worn benches sat beautiful young girls and handsome young men, all dressed in rich and colourful clothes, all cheerful, all talking and laughing amongst themselves as though they were having a good time. At the side musicians played exquisite music.

Gwynn looked down at the scene with satisfaction.

'Sit!' he said, his voice almost benign. 'Eat! Enjoy!'

There were places vacant and prepared for them near the head of the table, but not one of them moved towards them. Lukas felt strongly impelled to do so, but his recent experiences had taught him a great deal, and he resisted with all his strength.

'Sit!' commanded Gwynn ap Nudd, Lord of Annwn, once again, and the beautiful young people around the table fell silent and looked at the three strangers with growing resentment in their eyes.

Lukas, finding that the power of Gwynn's eyes was forcing him forward, exerted his own will to turn his back on him and walk towards the door. He half expected there to be an uproar at this, but there was no sound from behind him and he reached the doorway unmolested.

He took a step forward, longing for the fresh and lovely air he believed would greet him as he stepped through the dark portal. He wondered if Collen and Creiddylad were following him. The sooner they left this enchanted place the better!

But as he stepped out through the door he had entered no more than a few moments before, he gasped. Where there had once been a landscape of forested islands, flowering reed beds and water, he now saw a city that stretched to every horizon. Where there had been trees, there now were buildings. Where there had been living light reflected off water, there was now harsh, dead light reflected off glass. Huge chimneys belched steam and black smoke.

Nowhere did the people touch the earth. Nowhere did the people look to the sky.

A sound above him made him look up, and metal birds that roared flew across the sky in every direction, making so much noise that Lukas had to put his hands to his ears, and yet he could still feel the vibrations of their passing.

A movement behind him caused him to spin round and he found that Collen and Creiddylad and Gwynn were behind him looking at the changed world.

'But there is smoke between the people and the sky,' Lukas cried. 'How can they see the sun?'

'They do not need the sun,' said the King of Shadows triumphantly. 'I have given them heat. I have given them light. They can have heat and light at a touch. Why should they want the sun?'

'The earth,' Lukas said sadly. 'Where is the earth, the lovely growing green, the trees, the birds . . .?'

Gwynn laughed and his laugh was like the sound of thunder over distant mountains. Lukas looked desperately for some sign of the world as he had known it. He had never seen so many people, never dreamed of so many . . . thousands upon countless thousands . . . and from their city he could hear sounds . . . sounds of hooting, screeching, banging, roaring . . . voices babbling incessantly from boxes . . . music, wild and clashing, frantic music . . . each sound rising higher and higher to compete with the rest . . . until the people were encased in sound . . . encased in Gwynn's artifacts and gifts . . .

Of all the levels of Being that had once been man's reality, only the one was left – the material, the physical.

'See how happy they are,' said Gwynn. 'I have given them every-thing they want!'

And they were shown the faces of the people, and they could see that they were smiling, and laughing. But in their eyes there was something

Lukas had never seen in the eyes of the people he had known . . . boredom . . . emptiness . . . For all their possessions there seemed to be no satisfaction.

They had lost the memory of the earth and its subtle energies and its fine harmonies. They had lost the capacity to reach deep into a wisdom greater than their own. Even their language no longer had words through which the ancient mysteries could be remembered and understood.

Bitterly Creiddylad lifted her face to Gwynn's.

'You have cut them off from everything that comes to them from God and have forced them to live like blind maggots in a universe of splendours they cannot see.'

'That is only the beginning,' Gwynn said. 'When I am ready they will plead for me to give them the one thing they lack. A god. And when they plead I will answer them: "I am Gwynn: You are my people. Do you want *two* suns? I will *give* you two suns. Do you want to live inside a crystal ball? You shall live inside a crystal ball. Do you want a new universe? I will give you a new universe!" '

'A poor thing it will be!' Creiddylad said boldly. 'A universe, limited to your idea of what a universe should be!'

Gwynn's eyes flashed black fire. He lifted his arms like wings over her and they could feel the blast of his malevolence hot upon them.

'You have refused my feast and now you mock me,' he screamed. 'There is no room for you in my world!'

'Death was ever your kingdom,' she said quietly, holding her ground. 'But death used to be the gateway to a numinous land where the soul might rest before it continued its journey to the higher realms. Now you have become no better than those who fill us with the fear and dread of both life and death.'

The air roared around them with his rage.

'I'll show you!' he shrieked. 'I'll show you!'

He looked around wildly for something that would impress her. In the west the sun was lowering to the horizon. Magnificently its vast red bulk slid down the green and silent slopes of the domed heavens.

He stretched his arms above his head.

'I will change the motion of the sun!' he roared. 'Even the sun will obey me!'

They could see him straining his will towards the sun, his eyes fixed and staring. But still like liquid fire the great orb moved at its own pace, on its own course.

They saw his face distort with rage and disappointment, and they trembled to think what he might do in his frustration. But the effort must have depleted him, because instead of rounding on them as they were sure he would, he stood a while hunched and brooding, the sullen and shadowy centre of a whirlpool of deadly currents of energy.

They found they were free of the spell that before had made it so difficult for them to move against his wishes, and, had it not been for the currents that overlapped the summit and caught and flung them back, they might have prevailed at that moment against him.

Cerdic found the forest around him unaccountably dark. It was as though the sun had been suddenly extinguished in some way, and birds that had been singing moments before were now silent. He looked around himself uneasily. Something . . . something was very wrong. He was not in the forest at all but in a strange place, buildings such as he had never seen before rising taller than the tallest trees, stone and metal and glass where there had been trunks and branches and leaves, filthy tin cans and paper where there had been bracken and brambles. Weird sounds and sudden flashing lights bore in on him and he found himself dodging people who were pushing and jostling past him. A door opened and he heard shouting and banging. Suddenly a figure came hurtling through the door as though thrown by someone from inside. He looked down at the face, blood trickling from the side of a pale mouth. It reminded him of Matthew. Terrified, he looked up at the doorway and saw the red-faced thug who had put him there. It was his own face, older, coarser, stubble upon his chin, but unmistakably his own face.

He ran. He ran on the hard concrete and tarmac, down stinking alleyways where rats scavenged amongst rotting garbage and squealed at him as he passed. Someone threw a bottle at him which narrowly missed and shattered in a thousand lethal splinters on the wall beside his head.

He turned a corner and saw a group of dark figures beating a body on the ground. He tried to turn back, but they had seen him and abandoned the victim they already had for the new one they could see running from them. They cornered him against some mildewed boxes

104

and beat his head in. As he fell, trying to keep the kicking boots from blinding him, he knew that this must have been how Matthew felt . . .

'I am in hell,' he thought. 'I have died and I have gone to hell in punishment for what I have done to Matthew.'

On the top of the Tor the little group saw that the deep rich purple of the eastern sky above the layer of smoke had paled . . . and was beginning to shine and glow. It would not be long before the moon arose.

Gwynn saw it. He roused himself and turned towards it.

'The moon at least will obey me,' he muttered hoarsely. 'The moon shall not mock me!' He gathered himself together again, rising tall and as black as night. They could feel the waiting in the air . . . the tense holding back until the disc of silver should appear above the layer of fog.

Creiddylad raised her talisman in her right hand and her bough of glowing blossom in the left. Lukas saw her face flash with pain as she forced herself to move through the field of the sorcerer's dark energies and stand in front of him.

Both Lukas and Collen tried to move forward to help her, but they were flung back and lay groaning on the ground. Helplessly from there they watched the young woman standing before the fierce King of Shadows.

'Gwynn,' she said clearly, but Lukas caught the hint of a tremor in her voice.

In an instant Gwynn moved his gaze from the horizon to see who dared stand so close and call him by his name. His eyes sparked angrily to see that it was the woman who had rejected him.

Black fire suddenly flared up around them and crackled in the air.

Lukas cried out for the safety of the woman he loved, but, still held by an invisible force, he could do nothing to help her.

Mercifully, when the fire died down, she was still there, confronting Gwynn. He was lifting his hand against her in the gesture that Lukas had come to dread. The air around her was thick with acrid smoke and they could see she was holding her ground only with the greatest difficulty.

'Gwynn!' shouted Lukas desperately. He knew he could move no nearer, but he hoped his voice would cause a distraction. For a moment Gwynn wavered, and in that moment the girl gained strength visibly.

The moon rose. It swam in the clear dark sky like a shining swan, irradiating light from every magic feather.

The sorcerer forgot his opponent and turned his attention to the moon. He raised both his arms, his cloak of shadows billowing out so that its darkness covered all the land.

Creiddylad held her ground and lifted her stone of power high, the bough of blossom beside it in the other hand.

The moon beams found her in spite of Gwynn's dark cloak, and Lukas gasped to see them join the light that lifted from her shining face, giving it a power and splendour far beyond anything he had ever seen.

Across the huge and endless sky light moved and flashed. It seemed to him Gwynn's cloak swirled and flew, trying to break up the beams and rays of light and prevent them reaching the earth.

Who knows if he would have succeeded had Collen, Creiddylad and Lukas not found in their hearts the words of an ancient and powerful prayer they had believed they had forgotten.

Suddenly from the full circle of the horizon, above the black and ghastly fog, rose Shining Beings greater than the moon, more fiery than the sun. The transparent blue at the heart of any candle flame was dark to the light that swept and swirled across the horizon. Above it, arrows of white light swiftly rose, curved and fell in a shower of sparks, each one capable of turning the earth into an inferno beside which the mighty sun would seem a child's harmless toy. A wind of flame blew hard and fierce, crackling and howling . . . lightning stabbed and thrust . . . Nowhere in the violent beauty of the night could the Lord of Annwn hide.

Lukas shut and covered his eyes, but even through the lids and the thick bone of his hand, he could see the dazzle and sweep of light . . . the flurry of dark . . . and the final burst of brilliance.

He fell down on the earth and hid his face . . .

In the monastery that night Matthew fought for life. He had not been dead when Brother Peter carried him to the infirmary. All night long light and dark seemed to swirl and eddy around him. Sometimes he thought he heard voices, fine and high like the voices he imagined angels would have. At other times he heard harsh sounds and once he heard a scream that he thought he recognized.

'Cerdic,' he murmured, and Brother Peter who was sitting beside his bed leant forward at once and wiped his forehead with a cool damp cloth.

'Cerdic is not here child,' he said softly. 'Don't be afraid.'

'Cerdic,' whispered the boy again, and Brother Peter fancied that he heard no fear or hate in his voice, only pity. Tears came to his eyes. He had been sitting beside Matthew trying to pray, but finding that he could think of nothing but how much he disliked Cerdic. All his life Cerdic had enjoyed killing birds and insects and beasts – not just for food – but for pleasure. All his life he had terrorized anyone smaller or weaker than himself. It was as though the faculty of imagination, the eye of the soul, whereby the awareness of a person can leave its home and range freely amongst the rest of creation, seeing what others see, feling what others feel . . . was missing in Cerdic. Brother Peter knew that until Cerdic found this Eye in himself and learned to use it – he would stay the blind, stupid bully that he was.

It seemed to Cerdic that he lay a long time in a pool of his own blood, darkness and filth around him, pain in every limb. His tormentors had gone, no doubt thinking that he was dead.

'Please God – let me not be dead!' His mind said these words over and over again almost without his willing it. He was terrified of the hell the Abbot had described so vividly on so many occasions. He struggled to move his body but it would not move, he struggled to open his eyes but they would not open . . . he longed for the sunlight and the trees . . . the soft grass and the smell of herbs . . . and he even longed for the quiet routine of the monastery that had been so irksome to him before . . . anything . . . so long as it was life and away from this ghastly, soulless darkness that surrounded him. If only he could have the forgiveness the monks were always talking about . . . if only he could have another chance to start again . . .

'Matthew,' he whispered with a dry and rasping throat. 'Matt . . . if only I could give you your life again . . . if only . . .'

Lights began to flash around him. He could see them even through his closed lids . . . and the seeing brought unimaginable pain.

*   *   *

For how long Cerdic lay in this state he could not tell, but gradually the light began to lessen and the pain abate. He found he could open his eyes. He turned his head warily for it was still aching, and looked to see if he was still in that dark and stinking alley under the wall that shut out the sky. He was. But even as he groaned to think of it he heard a cracking sound and turned his head to look what it could be. He stared astonished. One of the flagstones on which he lay among the rotting garbage had cracked across and something was pushing through the crack. He dragged himself up to a sitting position, not taking his eyes off the crack for a moment, sickened and fearful as to what new horror was being prepared for him.

At first a small white thing that looked like a worm crawled out of the darkness from under the stone, but as it moved and grew larger every moment he realized that it wasn't a worm at all, but was an unfolding shoot. He gasped and now lent forward the better to see it. The shoot came up bent to protect itself and then began to unfold. Within moments he was staring at a small leaf on a sturdy stem. The rock was cracking further all the time. More leaves unfurled . . . the stem grew stronger . . . taller . . .

Other sounds attracted his attention and he turned his head. Everywhere he looked . . . the walls . . . the pavement . . . everything . . . was cracking open and the plant kingdom was reclaiming its own. He stood up and began to shout and jump with joy of seeing green leaves again. Walls began to tumble and he had to dodge and dart about . . . but he didn't care because all the time grass and trees were growing . . . darkness was lifting and the soft sunlight that he used to know was beginning to spread over everything . . .

18

WHEN LUKAS AT last dared to lift his head he too was astonished at what he saw. Three Beings of Light were upon the summit of the Tor, and there was no sign of the Lord of Annwn's palace, nor of the King of Shadows himself. Brother Collen was beside him and his face was glowing with awe and reverence.

'Who *are* they?' whispered Lukas, clutching the hermit's arm.

'One of them you know,' he answered softly.

Lukas stared but did not recognize any of them.

'You know her as the Lady Creiddylad,' Collen whispered.

Lukas saw now that it was she, the girl he loved, but now transformed . . . the Mother of the Earth, the bringer of Life and renewal . . . The Green Lady in full glory.

'How beautiful,' he thought, and his heart ached to see such beauty.

'The others?' he whispered to Brother Collen.

'That one I think is Gabriel, the Angel of Revelation.'

Lukas trembled. The deep blue of the cloak worn by Gabriel was the colour of the sky before full dawn, transparent and glowing. As he moved silver and green flows of light gleamed through it.

Lukas turned to the other and his heart leapt. The Angel Mik-hael, the destroyer of demons, the champion of the Lord Christ. His sword forged in the white heat of the human heart. His face too bright to look upon. His stature beyond human comprehension.

Now Lukas watched him turn to leave, and, with the movement of his shoulder, it was as though the rising sun was lifted from behind the earth and its golden splendour pulled across the sky . . . his cloak of flame, the sunrise . . .

Lukas hardly dared to breathe. He stared and stared . . . trying to drink everything in and hold it to himself. The night had passed and he had not noticed it. What he had once known of time, of reality and of illusion, no longer made sense.

Brother Collen touched Lukas' arm. He too was trembling.

Lukas looked at him and followed his pointing finger to the landscape below the Tor.

Like an evil dream Gwynn's mess was gone. The lovely earth was green again, the waters gold and red with the reflection of the dawn. A lark rose from the forest and hung above their heads . . . singing . . .

But Gwythyr's heart still ached for the woman he had loved. Great spirit she might be – but he had known her as woman.

And then they found her, a frail, spent figure, a lady of great age. She lay curled like a wisp of smoke, scarcely breathing. He leant over her; he stroked her silver hair, her soft cheek.

Faintly she shook her head. 'You must not mourn for me,' she whispered. 'You have a new life to live and I will never be far away. Once out of time and space there is no far and near, after or before . . .'

He kissed her gently knowing that it was for the last time as Gwythyr and Creiddylad, as Lukas and the Lady of the cavern. She looked past his head to Collen.

'Gwynn's scheme has not won through this time,' she said faintly. 'But keep watch: it doesn't need a power-crazed sorcerer to bring it about: the dark side of the human heart is a perpetual challenge to the light.'

Her eyes closed. She was slipping away from them.

'Stay,' Lukas cried hoarsely. 'I cannot live without you! Stay. Please stay!'

But her earth-body was dead: her last breath a sigh.

Lukas drew back from her. Collen put his arm around his shoulder.

'What now?' Lukas asked sadly. After such a night how could they live as before?

Collen shook his head and was silent. So much had happened: so many forces were at work in their lives. It seemed to him that the Abbot represented as dark a force as Gwynn. He demanded obedience to a god he did not understand. 'Not for love,' Collen thought, 'not for love he asks us to give up self – but for fear.' The two had so much power, so much potential for good, yet they turned it against the flow, the rhythm of the universe. 'Two of a kind,' he muttered, 'each missing the point of his own religion.' Each paying too much attention to the physical realm. One to manipulate it by imposing unnatural disciplines on the body, the other to manipulate it by using magic – both forgetting that it is the questing individual spirit and its urge to evolve and grow at its own pace and in its own way that keeps the universe on course and in harmony with its timeless purpose.

'It is up to us now,' he said aloud and shook himself free of moody speculation. 'We have been given a fresh start and we must make the most of it.'

Lukas pointed to the pewter bottle at his belt.

'You did not use the holy water after all,' he said. 'Would it not be fitting to pour it out upon the Tor as a kind of . . . offering and . . . a kind of cleansing?'

Brother Collen took the pewter bottle from his belt and held it high. Lukas watched as it flowed like liquid crystal through the clear air and seeped into the grass. When the last drop was gone, they smiled at each other, feeling that the Tor at least was now clear of Gwynn's dark dream.

'We should bury her,' Lukas said now, looking at the figure of the grey lady.

'Aye.'

As they stooped to lift her they noticed that the amber had been shattered by the strength of the forces that had fought around it all night long, and it lay now in a small pile of flame coloured dust beside her.

Lukas scooped it up in his hands and blew upon it, so that it took to the air and drifted with the breezes of the morning to lie at last scattered upon the land.

When he turned back to her, she too was dust, and there was nothing left to bury.

They looked around them. It was as though nothing had happened. The sun was settled into its daily path, and the air was warming nicely. In a field not far from the edge of the forest a herd of cows was being driven out by a farmer's boy. Lukas could see a horse and its foal, and people far below on the road, going to market.

In the infirmary Matthew opened his eyes and smiled.

SOURCES

1) For the story of the confrontation of Gwynn ap Nudd and the Christian hermit, Saint Collen:
   LIVES OF THE BRITISH SAINTS (Life of Saint Collen)
   S. Baring Gould. Pub. John Hodges, London 1875
   THE MABINOGION by Lady Charlotte Guest (note to p. 100)
   Pub. J. M. Dent & Co 1906
   GLASTONBURY TOR: A GUIDE TO THE HISTORY AND LEGENDS by Nick Mann
   Pub. Annenterprise 1986
   Gwynn ap Nudd was called 'the king of the fairies' in the story of Saint Collen. Fairies in Celtic times and the Dark Ages were often the result of race memories of a people who had lived long, long before; a people powerful and magical, capable of magnificent transformations and illusions; associated with stone circles, with timelessness, with mazes and with earth mounds: a people whose knowledge of other realities and whose deeds of magic and transformation had become exaggerated and feared over the centuries.

2) For the story of Gwynn ap Nudd's relationship with Gwythyr, son of Greidyawl, and Creiddylad:
   THE MABINOGION by Lady Charlotte Guest (note to p. 100 and the story of 'Kilhwch and Olwen')
   THE MABINOGION by Jeffrey Gantz (the story of 'How Culhwch won Olwen' ps. 159, 167, 168)
   Pub. Penguin 1976

3) For legends about a tunnel under the Tor:
   'GLASTONBURY TOR: a guide to the history and legends' by Nick Mann
   Pub. Annenterprise 1986

'GLASTONBURY MAKER OF MYTHS' by Frances Howard-Gordon
Pub. Gothic Image 1982
Article by Ann Pennick in 'GLASTONBURY, ANCIENT AVALON, NEW
JERUSALEM' edited by Anthony Roberts
Pub. Rider 1978

4) For the story of the Green Lady or Earth Goddess imprisoned in
the Tor (the 'Persephone connection'), first mentioned in the
biography of Gildas written by Caradoc of Llancarfan in connec-
tion with Guinevere's kidnapping and imprisonment by King
Melwas of Somerset, see Geoffrey Ashe: AVALON, THE STORY OF
GLASTONBURY (Fontana 1977), and THE QUEST FOR ARTHUR'S BRITAIN
(Paladin 1968). In GLASTONBURY TOR: A GUIDE TO THE HISTORY AND
LEGENDS Nick Mann writes: 'Returning to Caradoc's story of
Melwas, and his imprisonment on the Tor of Guinevere and the
ensuing struggle with Arthur, interesting things occur when it is
compared with the story of the rivalry between Gwynn and
Gwythyr for Creiddylad. . . . The mythical quality of the whole
increases when it is clear that in both cases Creiddylad and
Guinevere are daughters of a solar king. . . .

'If the Arthur and Melwas story is an update of the earlier Celtic
legend of Gwynn and Gwythyr, and if Caradoc had good reasons
from his sources for locating the struggle on the Tor (the legend of
St Collen makes it clear that Gwynn at least was to be found there),
then we may have a glimpse of Celtic and pagan beliefs surrounding
the symbolic nature of the Tor.

'We may speculate that the Tor was the scene of some great
fertility ritual at the beginning of May, where the powers of Earth
and Heaven struck a balance to ensure the return of the sun and the
continuation of the cycle of the year.'

The 'Persephone connection' is also implicit in the Great
Mother, Earth Goddess link with Glastonbury Tor drawn by
Frances Howard-Gordon in her book GLASTONBURY MAKER OF
MYTHS. Pub. Gothic Image 1982

5) Glastonbury Isle as the entrance to the Celtic Otherworld is
mentioned by many authors including Geoffrey Ashe in CAMELOT
AND THE VISION OF ALBION (Panther 1973)

6) The Otherworld itself as a golden land entered through a passage between crystal trees after a boat ride over water is well described in EARLY IRISH MYTHS AND SAGAS by Jeffrey Gantz. Pub. Penguin 1981

7) The shaman's bag of crane-skin: KELTIC FOLK AND FAERIE TALES by Kaledon Naddair. Pub. Rider 1987: 'Keltic Druids kept their Koelbren lots, their Ogham "Cranchann" within a crane/heron skin bag.' Cranes are related to 'the young goddess of Fertility' and to those who 'preside over the mysteries of reincarnation . . .'

8) The perpetual choir of Glastonbury monastery is mentioned in the Welsh Triads and by Geoffrey Ashe in CAMELOT AND THE VISION OF ALBION

9) For Gwynn's challenge of the stars see: JOHN DEE: THE WORLD OF AN ELIZABETHAN MAGUS by Peter J. French. Pub. RKP 1972 (p. 116). '. . . the religious magus could theoretically change the stars and control the heavenly powers. But the strain would be so great that his body would be destroyed and his spiritual essence would be completely absorbed into the Godhead. This great transformation was exactly what Dee was attempting through his magic.'

I cannot give every source from a lifetime of reading – but these are the most recent I have consulted.

GOTHIC IMAGE PUBLICATIONS

We are a Glastonbury based imprint dedicated to publishing books and pamphlets which offer a new and radical approach to our perception of the world in which we live.

As ideas about the nature of life change, we aim to make available those new perspectives which clarify our understanding of ourselves and the Earth we share.

Leylines and Ecology: An Introduction
William Bloom & Marko Pogacnik — £1.95

Devas, Fairies and Angels: A Modern Approach
William Bloom — £2.95

Glastonbury – Maker of Myths
Frances Howard-Gordon — £4.50

Spiritual Dowsing
Sig Lonegren — £4.95

Needles of Stone Revisited
Tom Graves — £6.50

Meditation in a Changing World
William Bloom — £6.50

Dragons – Their History and Symbolism
Janet Hoult — £4.50

Also available from Gothic Image

DRAGONQUEST

Filmed on a Gothic Image Magical Britain Tour, this unique 45-minute production explores the origin and meaning of the ancient sacred sites of the British Isles including Stonehenge, Avebury, Castle Rigg and the Merry Maidens, in addition to Neolithic stone circles and ruins of early Christian churches. We visit perennial centres of pilgrimage such as Glastonbury, Iona and Lindisfarne.

Some of Britain's leading writers and scholars appear at the locations and give their insight into legend, history and mysterious earth energies. Pagan gods and goddesses, Merlin, King Arthur, dragons, ancient forces and powers of seership are discussed and revealed.

The remarkable ground and aerial photography has many scenes of extraordinary beauty as well as unique graphics and illustrations. Original music by Bob Stewart (UK) and Jim Oliver (USA) invoke the spirit of ancient sites throughout the film. The fusion of images, research, music, integrity and inspiration generate a powerful enchanting experience. Available and compatible for UK and USA buyers on VHS only. £27.50